A.L.I.E.E.E.N.

LEWiS TRONDHEiM

A.L.I.E.E.E.N.

ARCHIVES of LOST ISSUES and EARTHLY EDITIONS
of EXTRATERRESTRIAL NOVELTIES

First Second

NEW YORK & LONDON

It was mid-April 2006. Around 12:30 PM. I was with my wife and children on vacation in the Catskills, looking for a nice picnic spot.

We had been hiking awhile when we came upon a shady grove that seemed ideal to sit and have our salami and chips.

On closer look, I noticed the grass had been burned and I cursed such insensitive backpackers. Not only that, bits of debris were littered everywhere. We were about to turn around and head back when I spotted a tattered, beaten-up comic book on the ground. I turned it over with my foot, to peek at its cover. I recognized neither the artist, nor the title, nor even the alphabet it was in.

Just about then I felt a rush of excitement that bordered on panic. I looked again at the markings on the ground — and no doubt about it, the singed grass was shaped in a perfect circle. And the miscellaneous bits and pieces left behind had obviously not been made locally, nor in this country, nor even on Earth.

After reading the comic book, which was pretty badly weatherworn, I got in touch with First Second and submitted what appears to be the very first comic strip for extra-terrestrial children ever discovered on our planet.

Since then, I've been combing the hills to find other evidence of these sloppy campers.

Lewis Trondheim

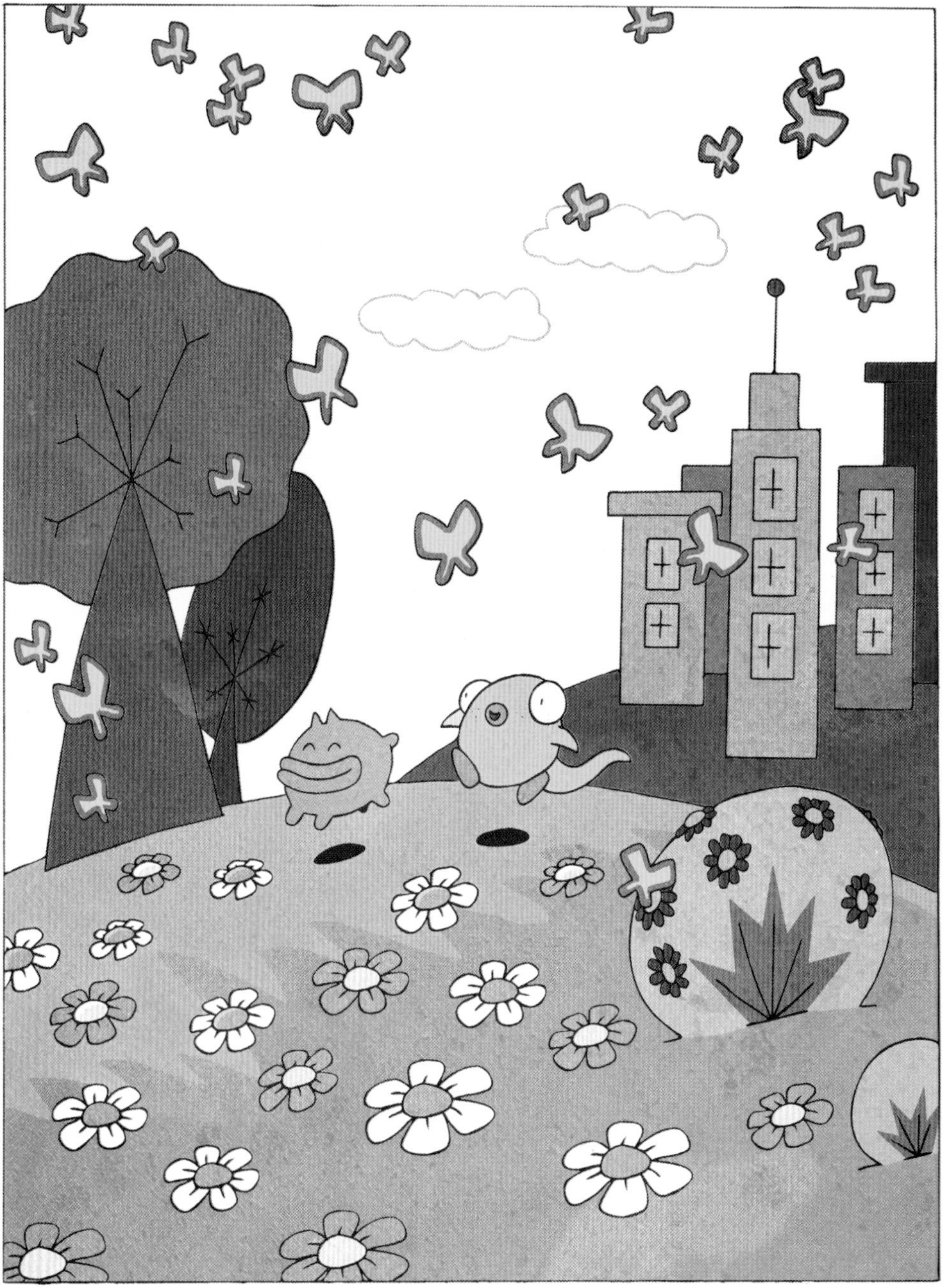

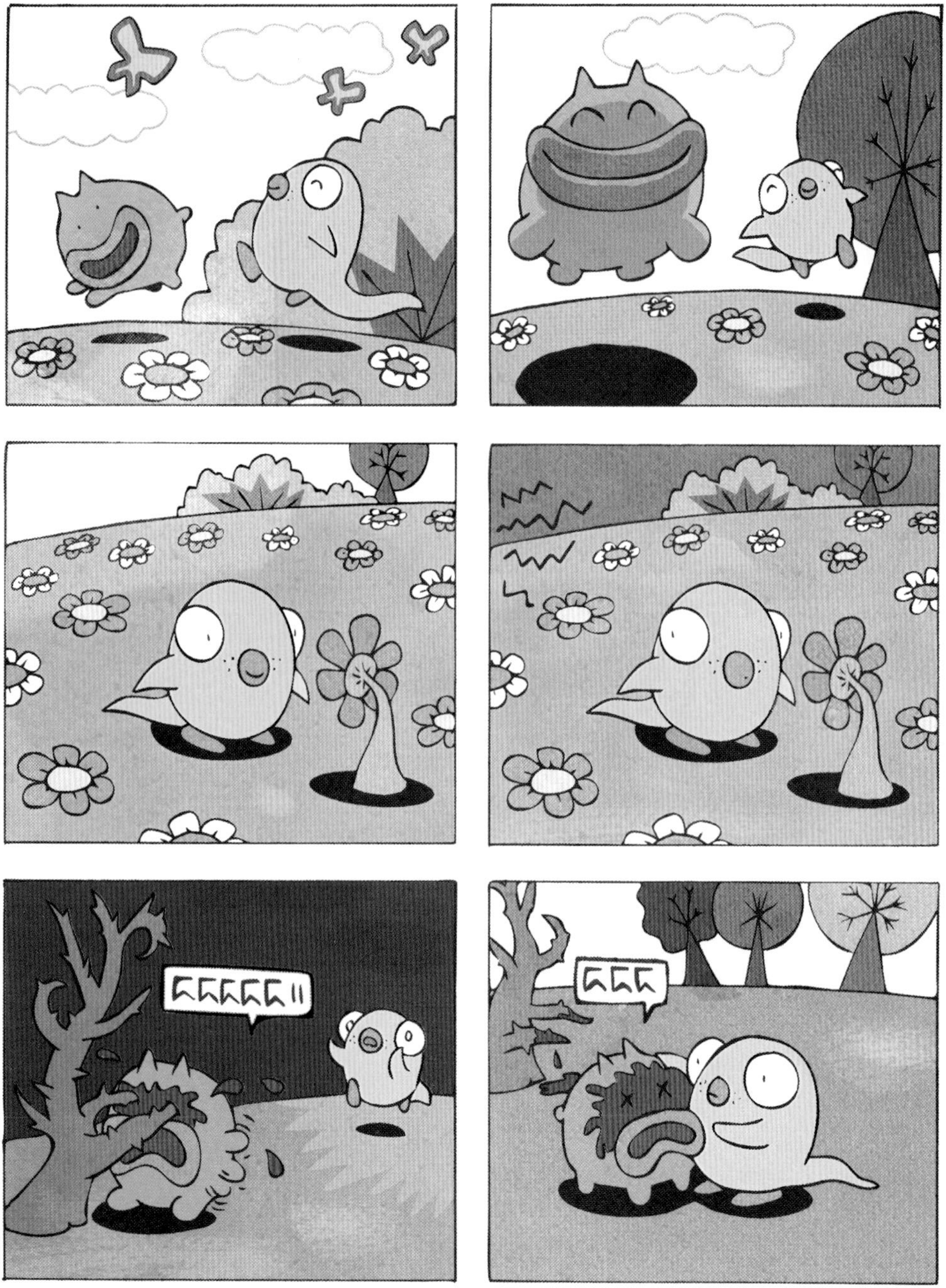

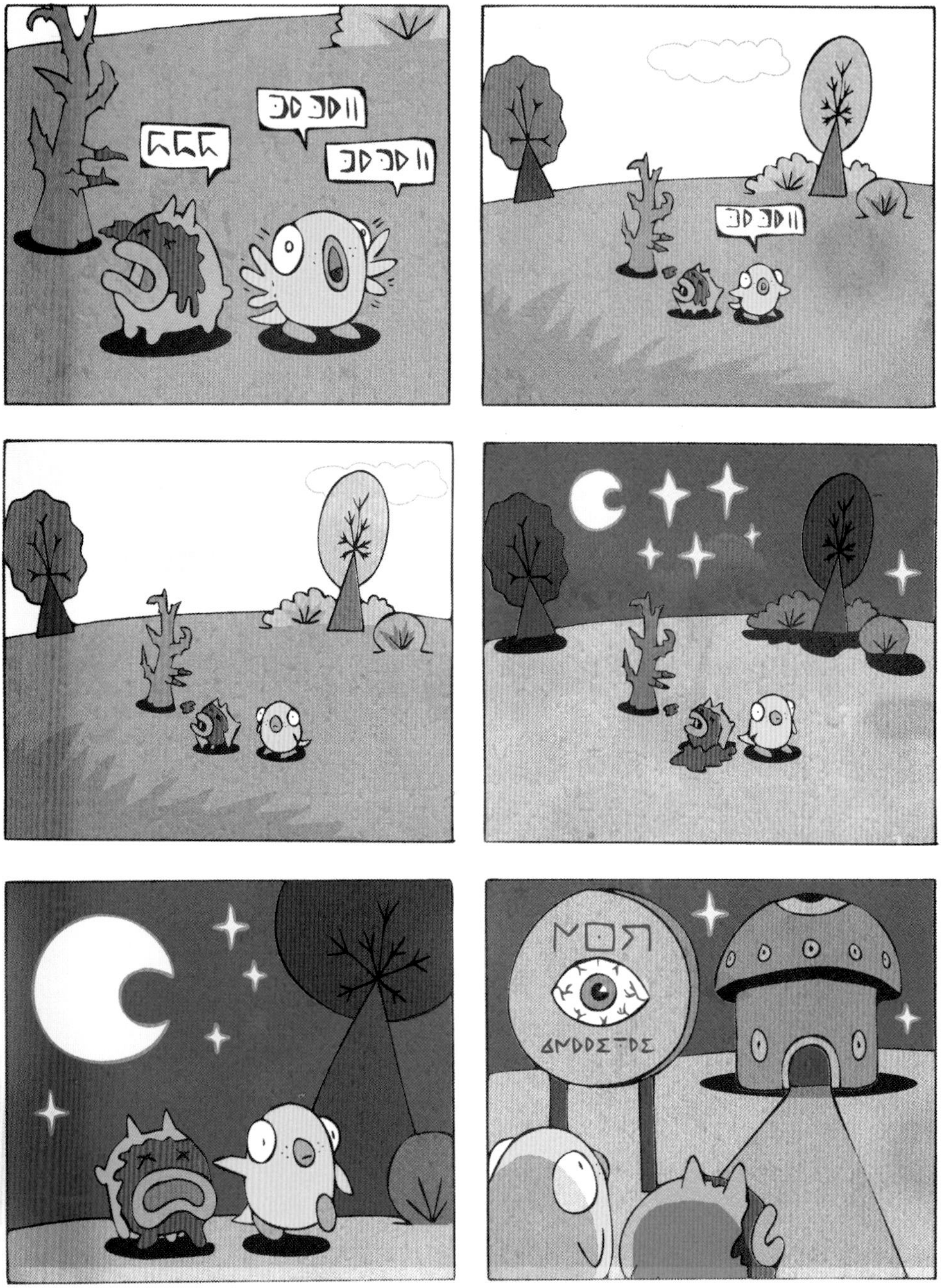

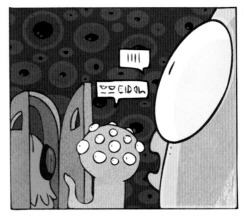

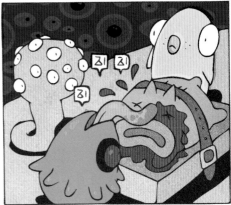

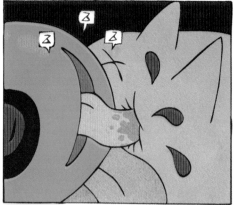

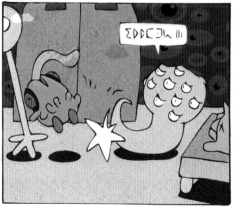

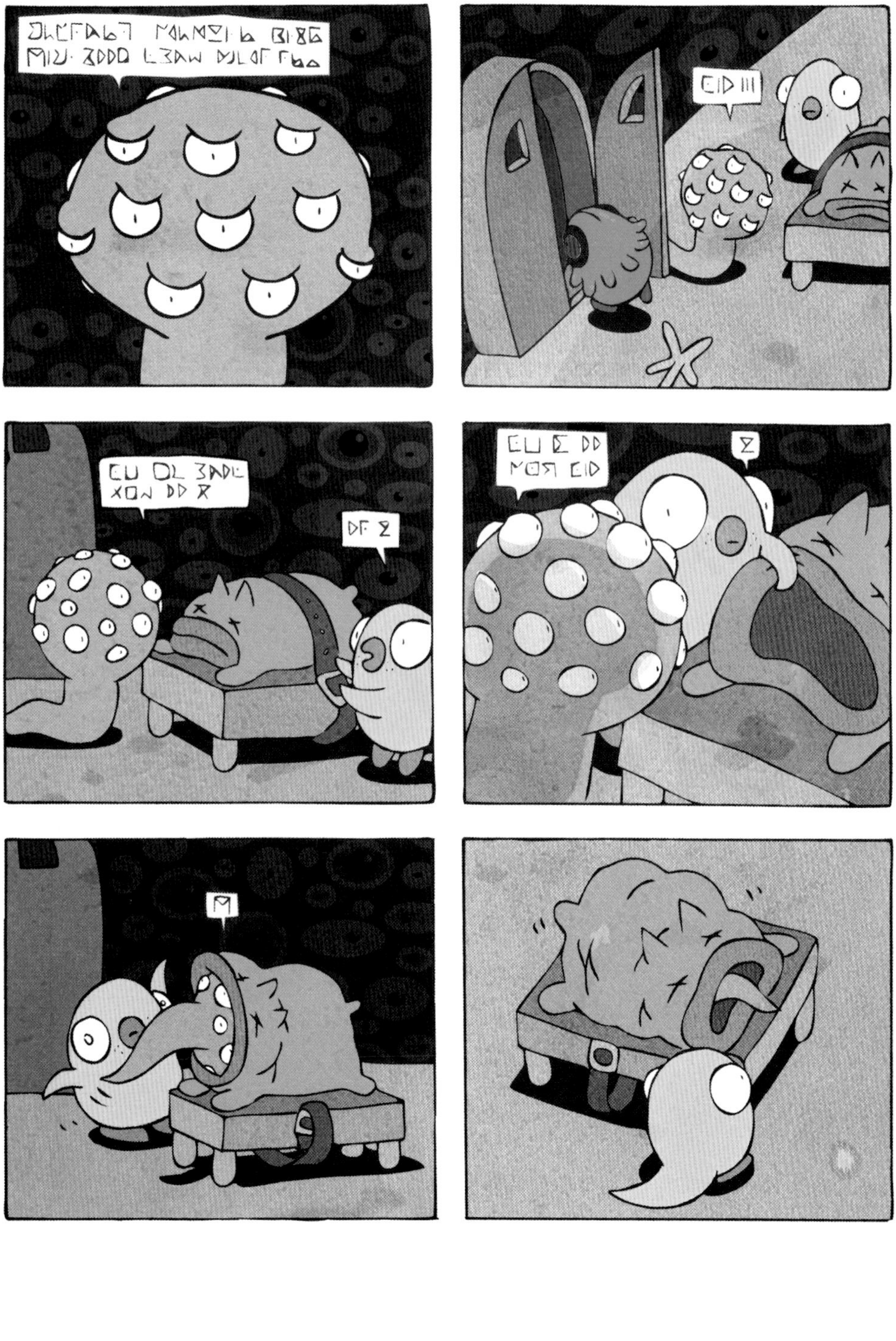

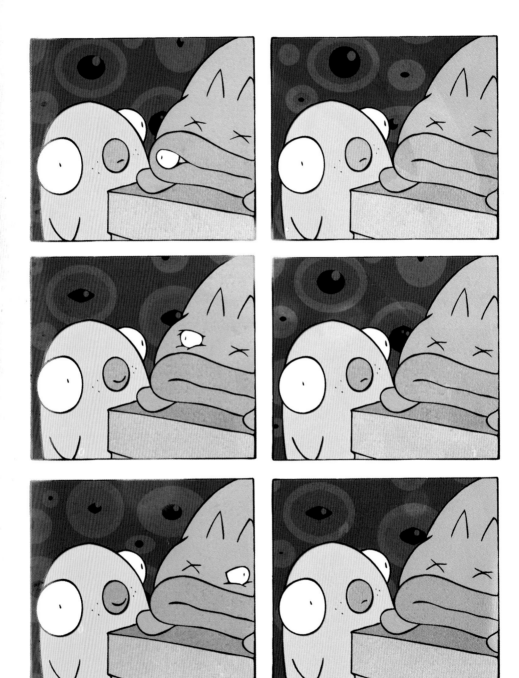

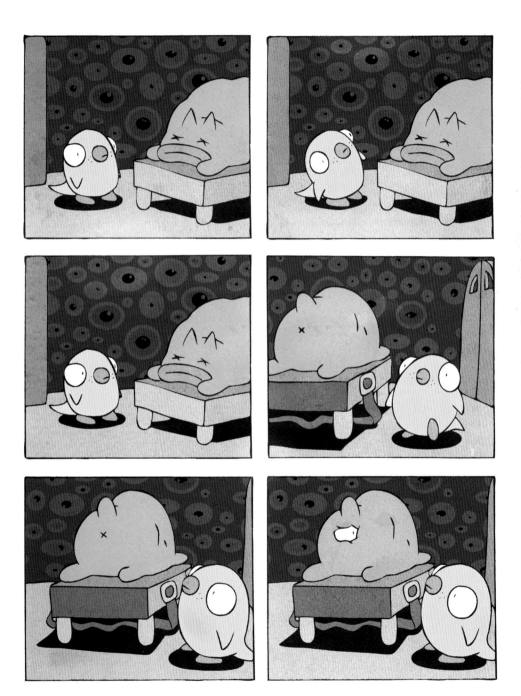

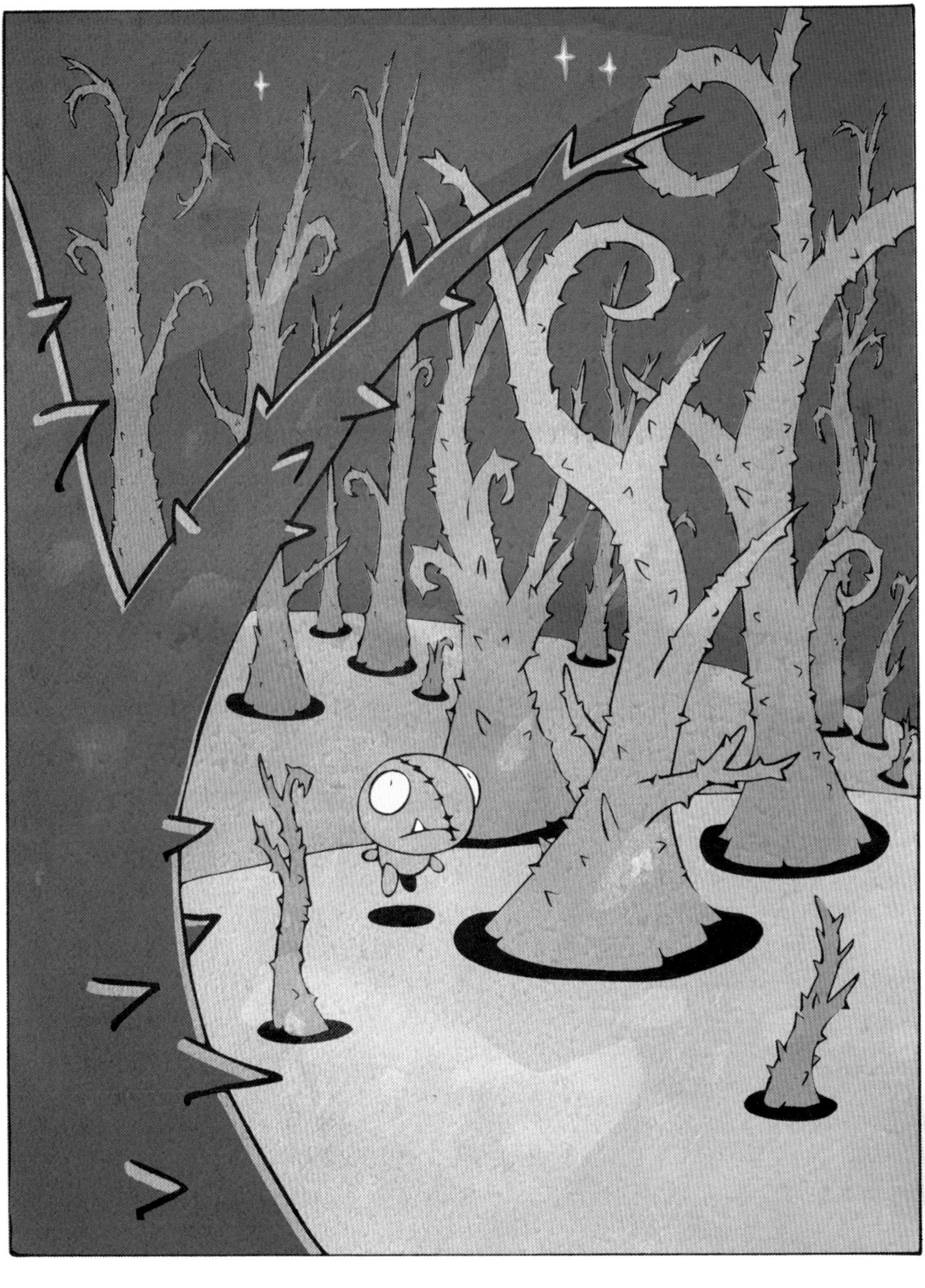

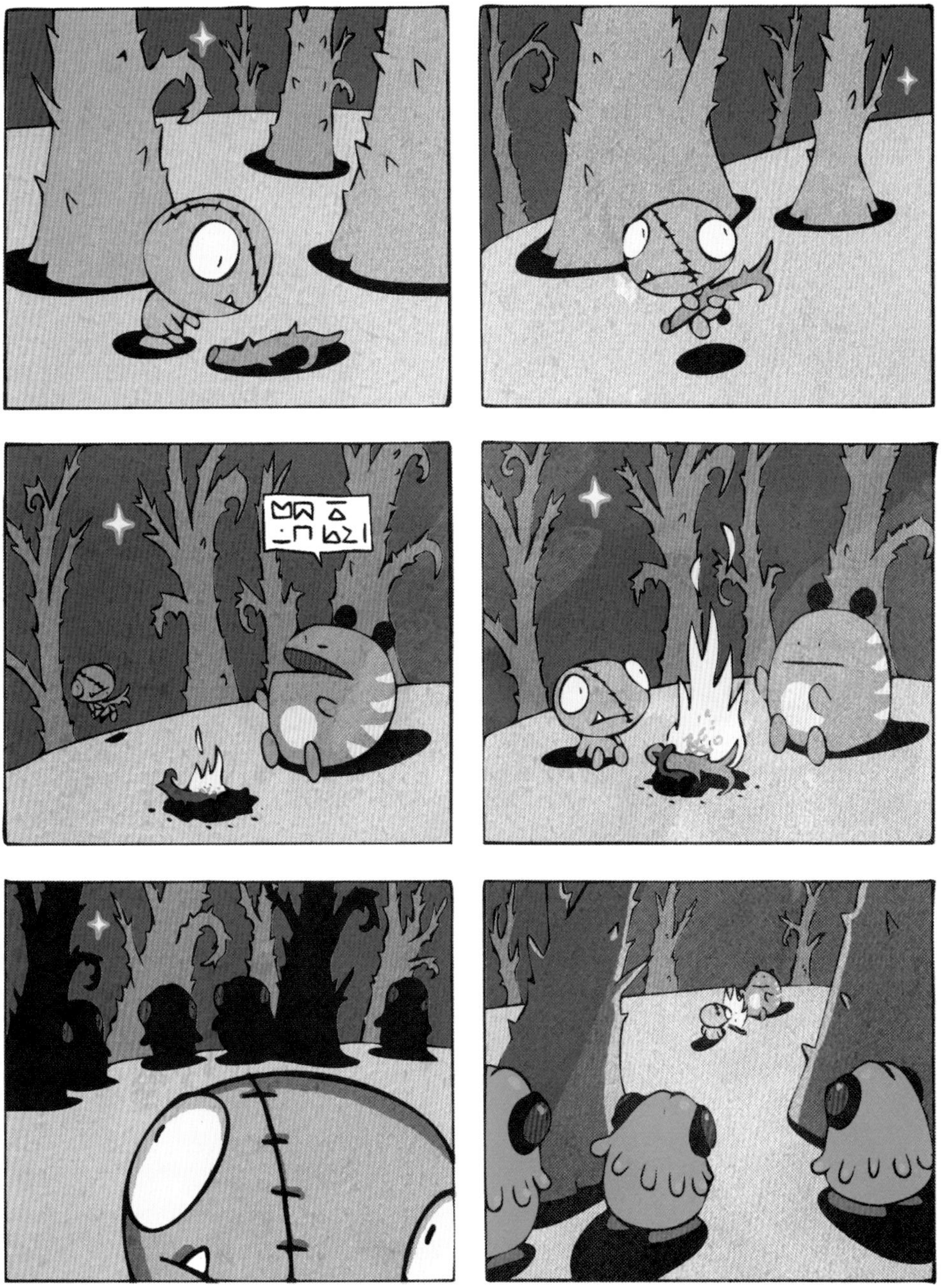

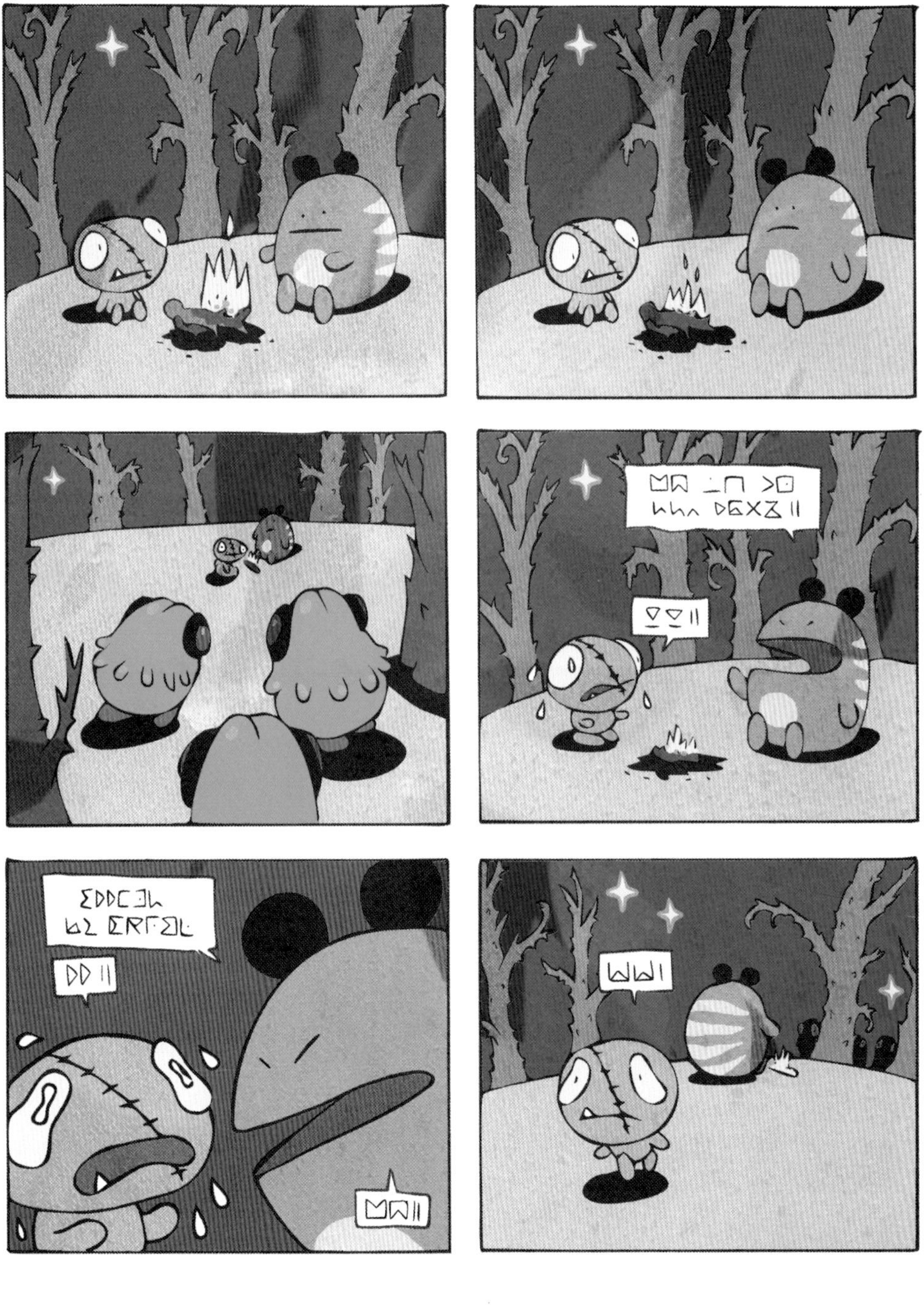

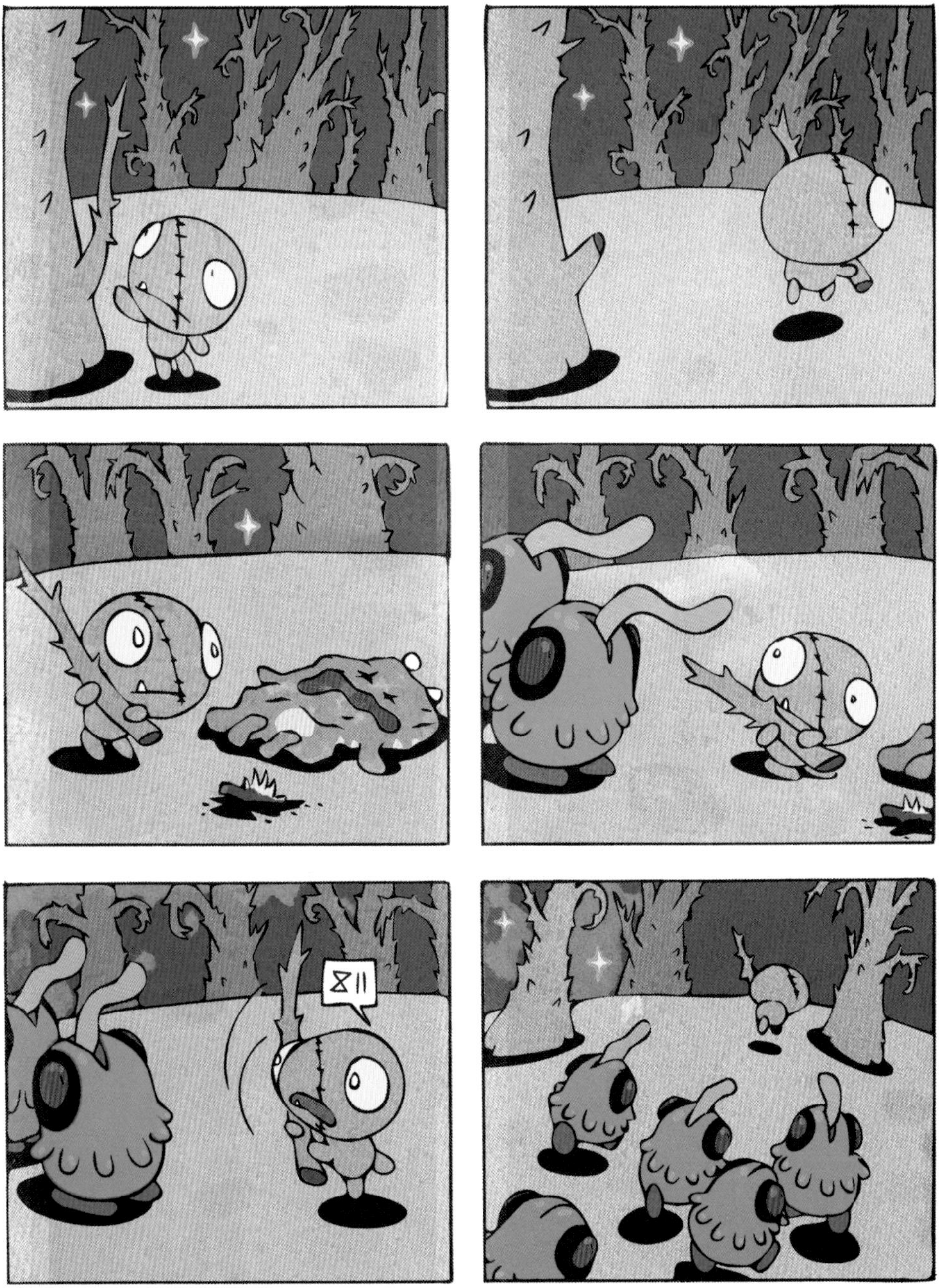

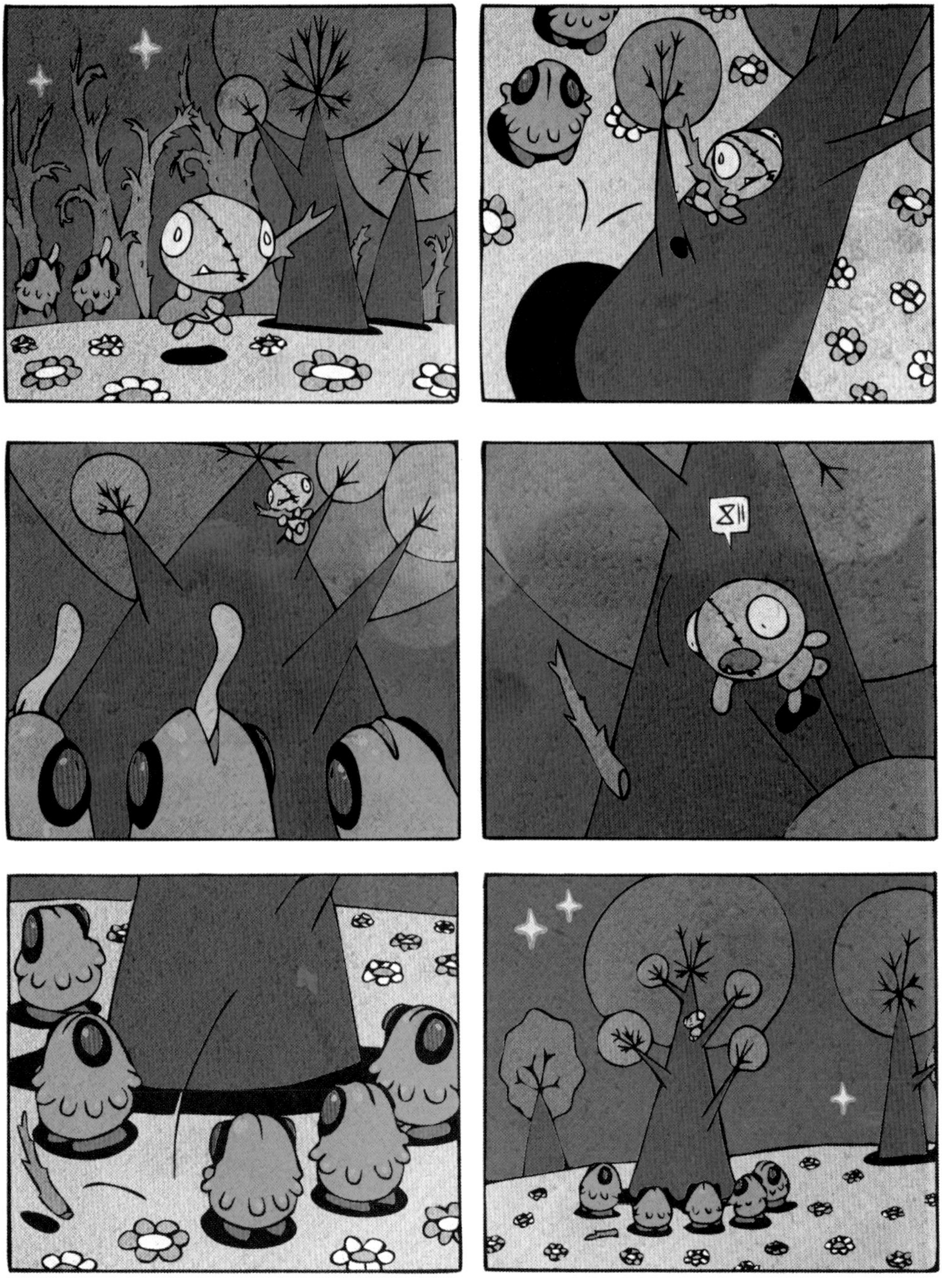

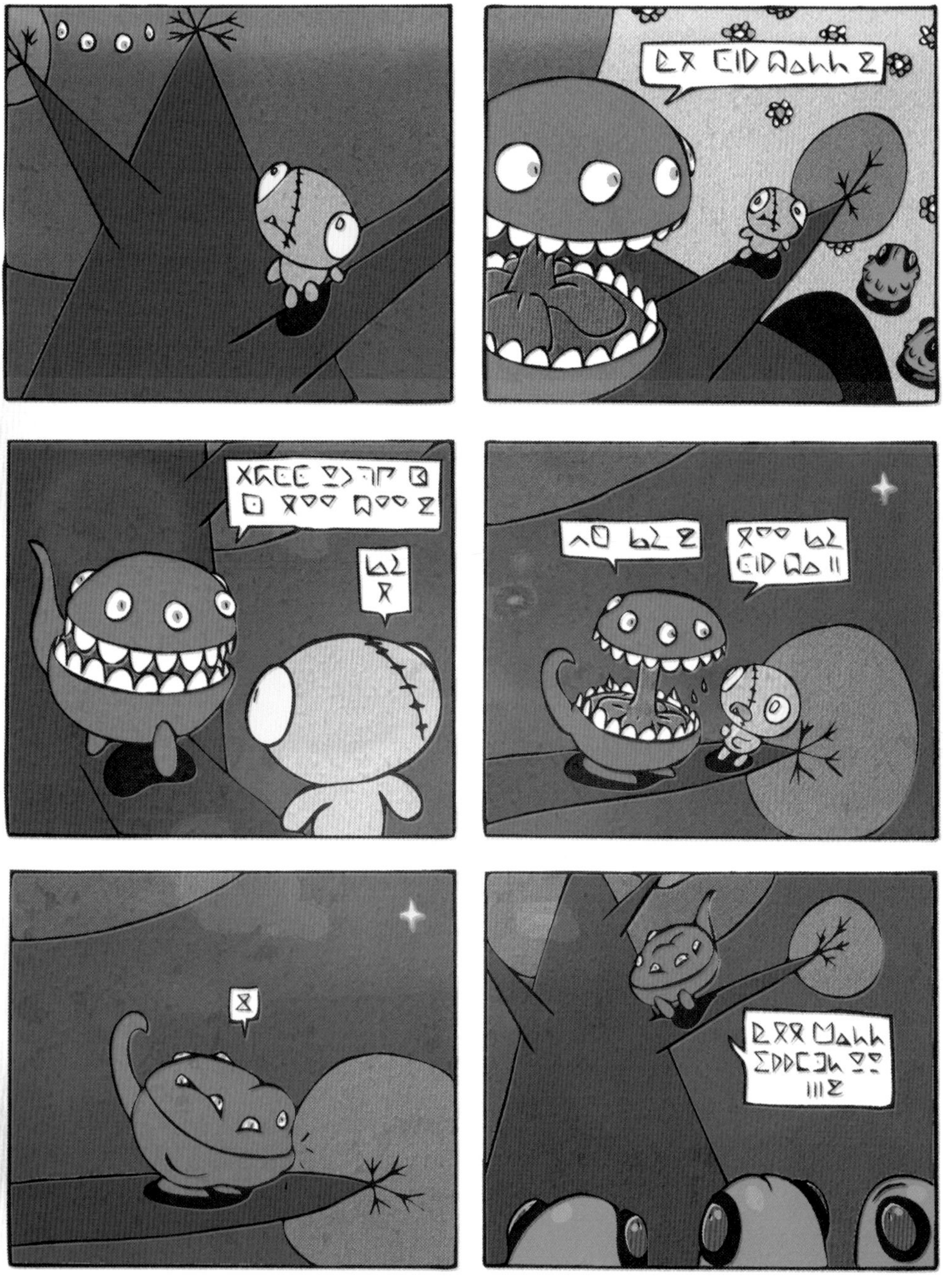

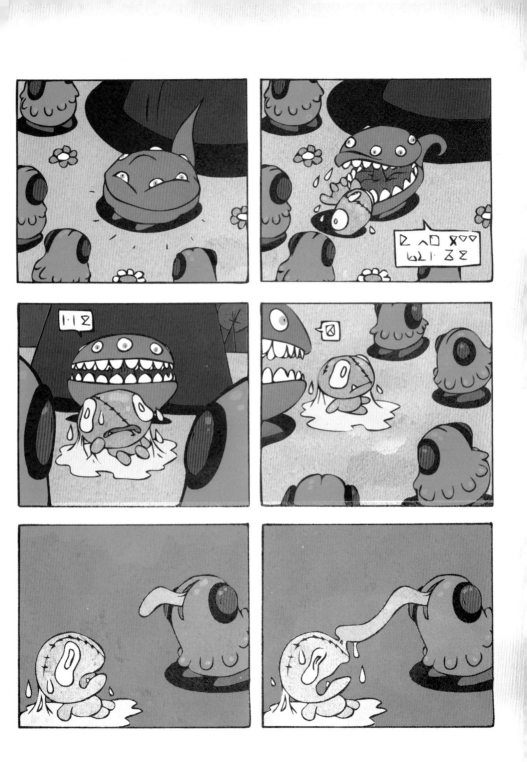

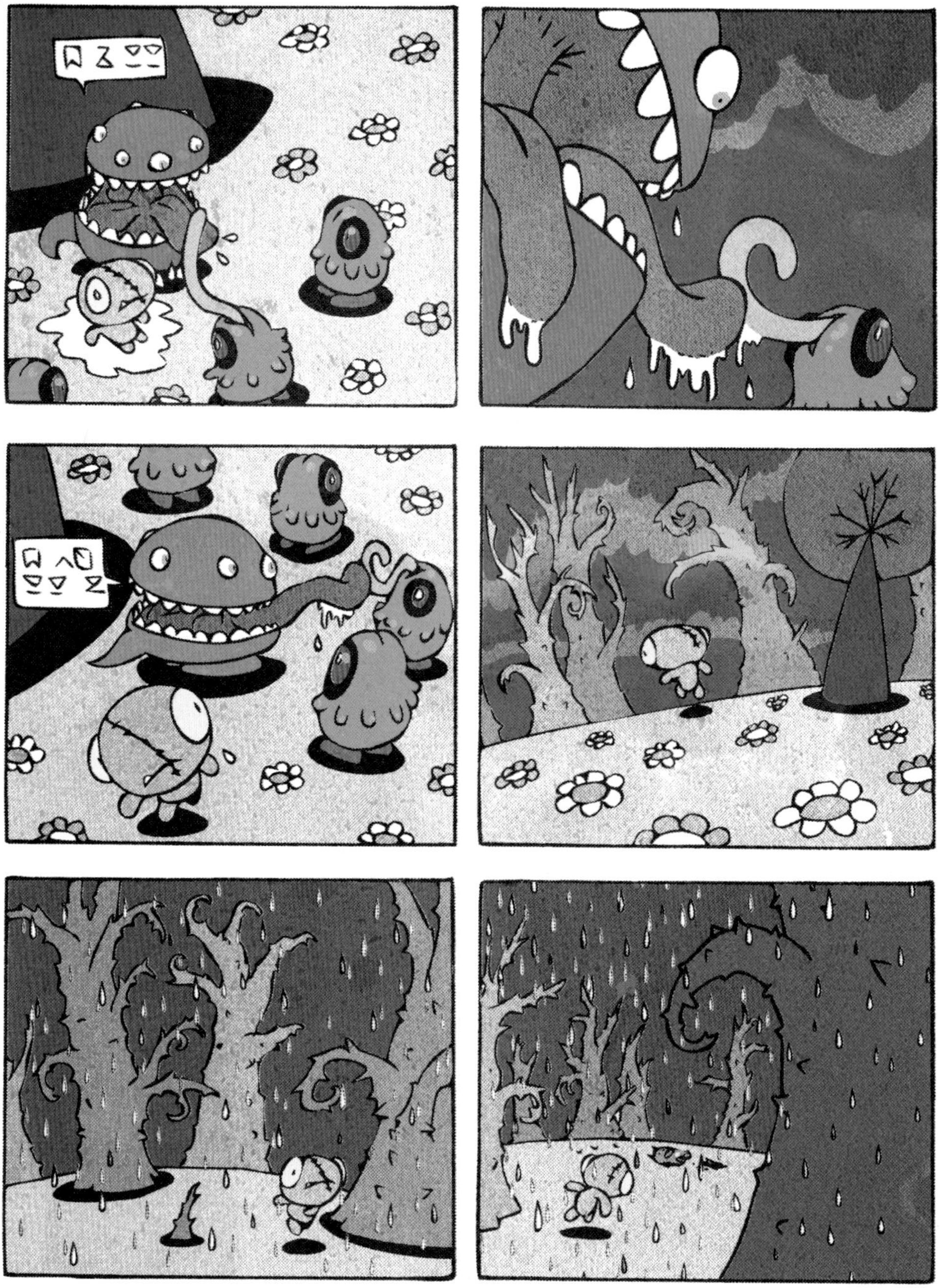

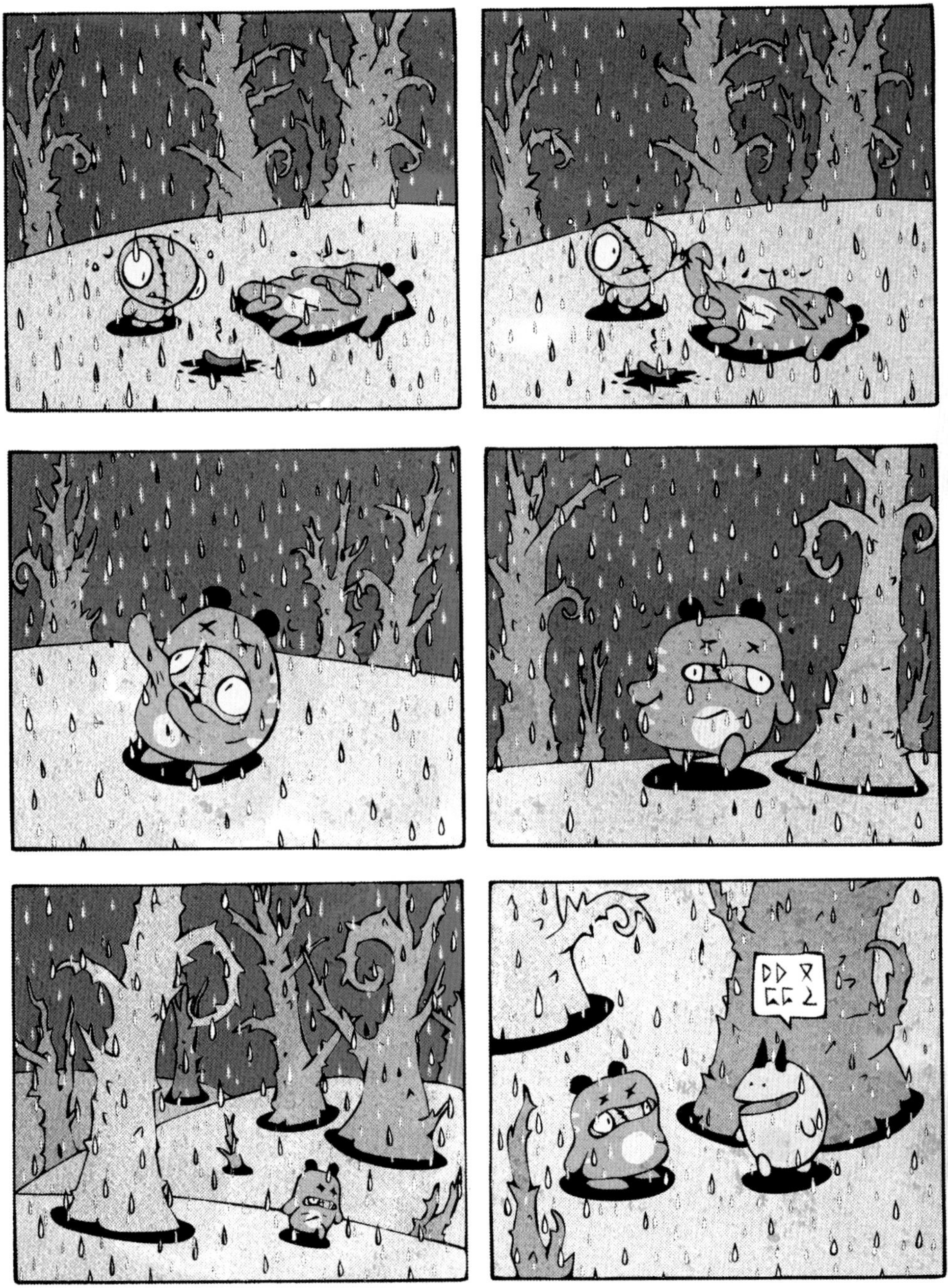

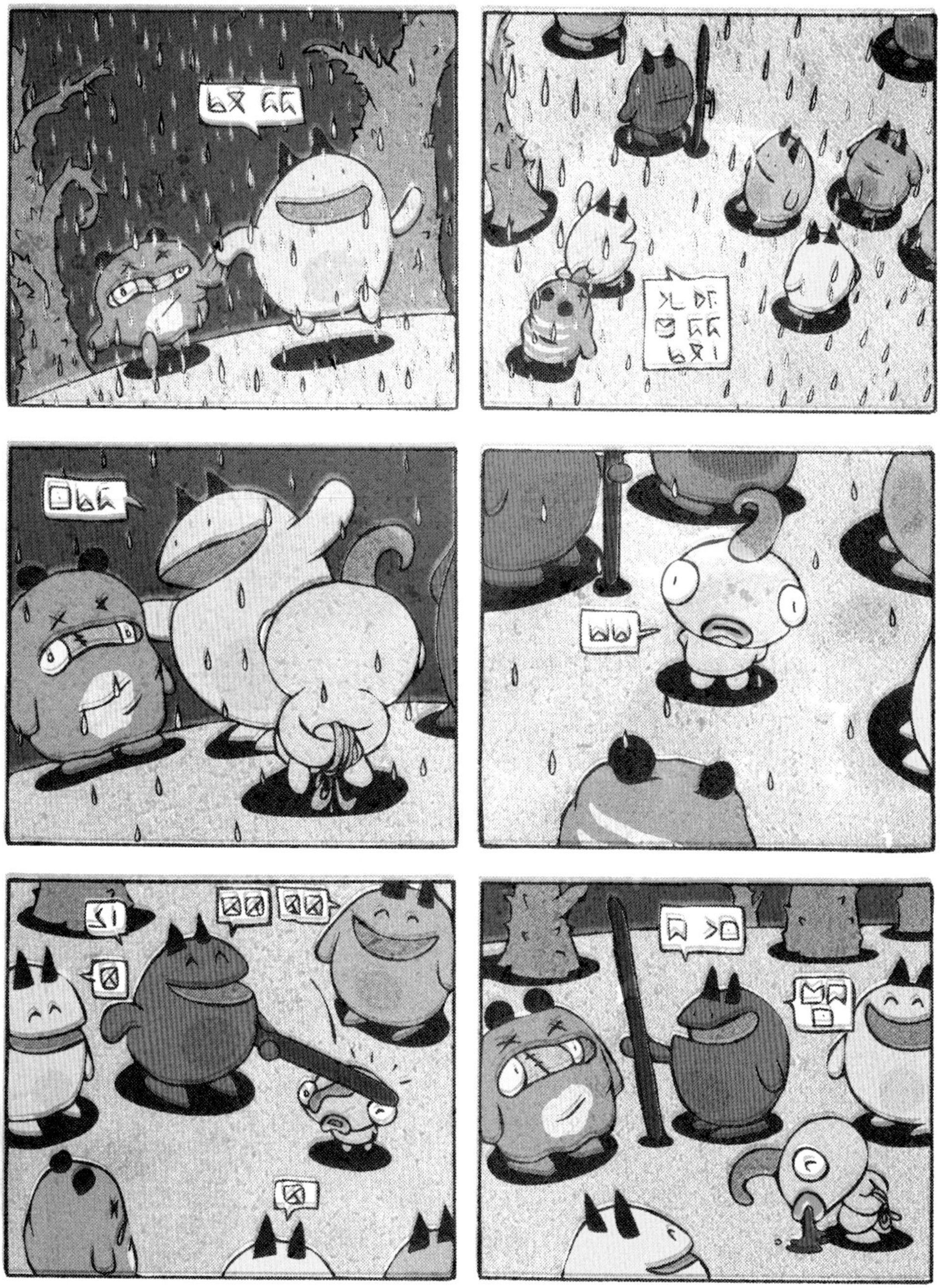

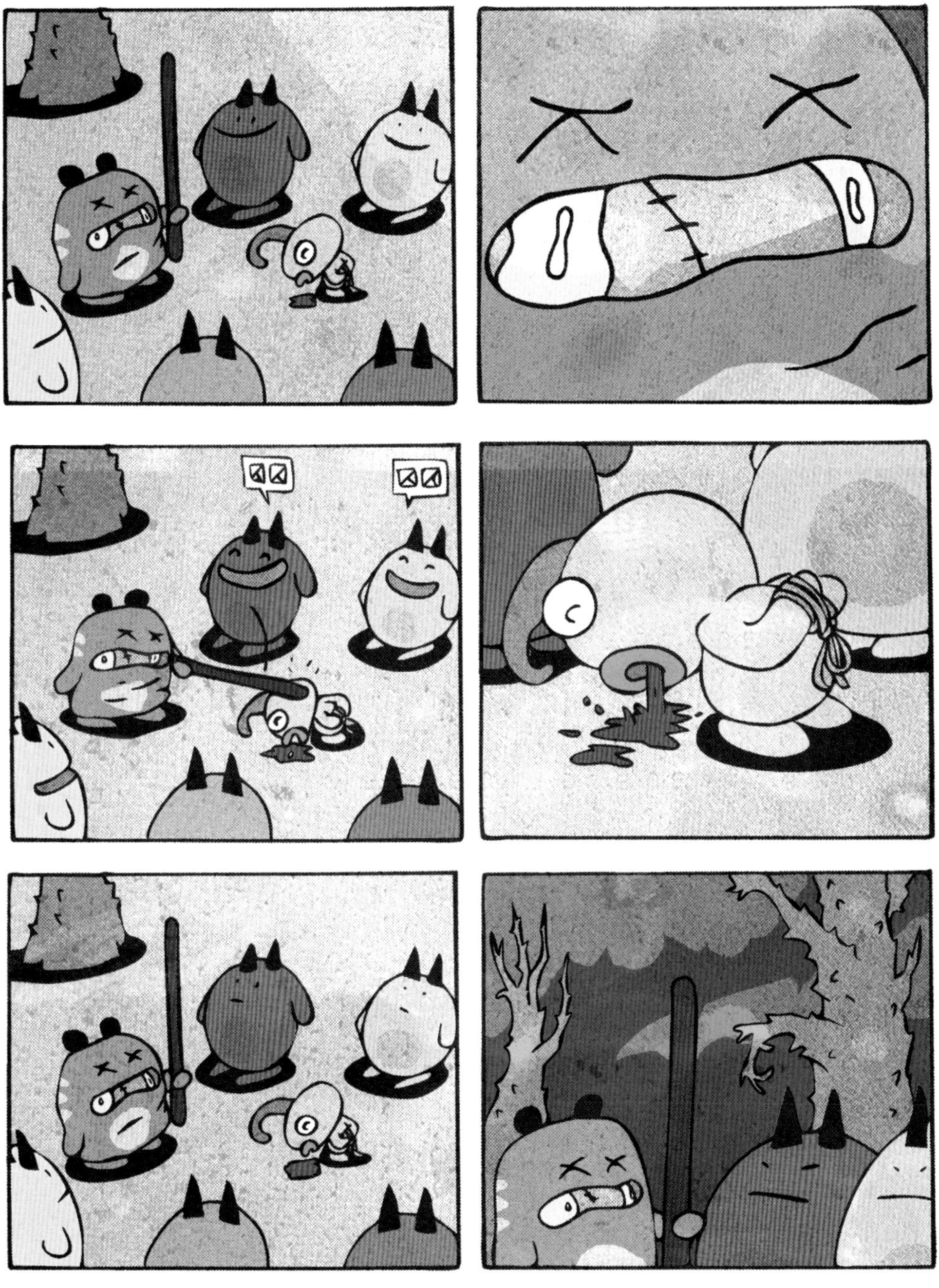

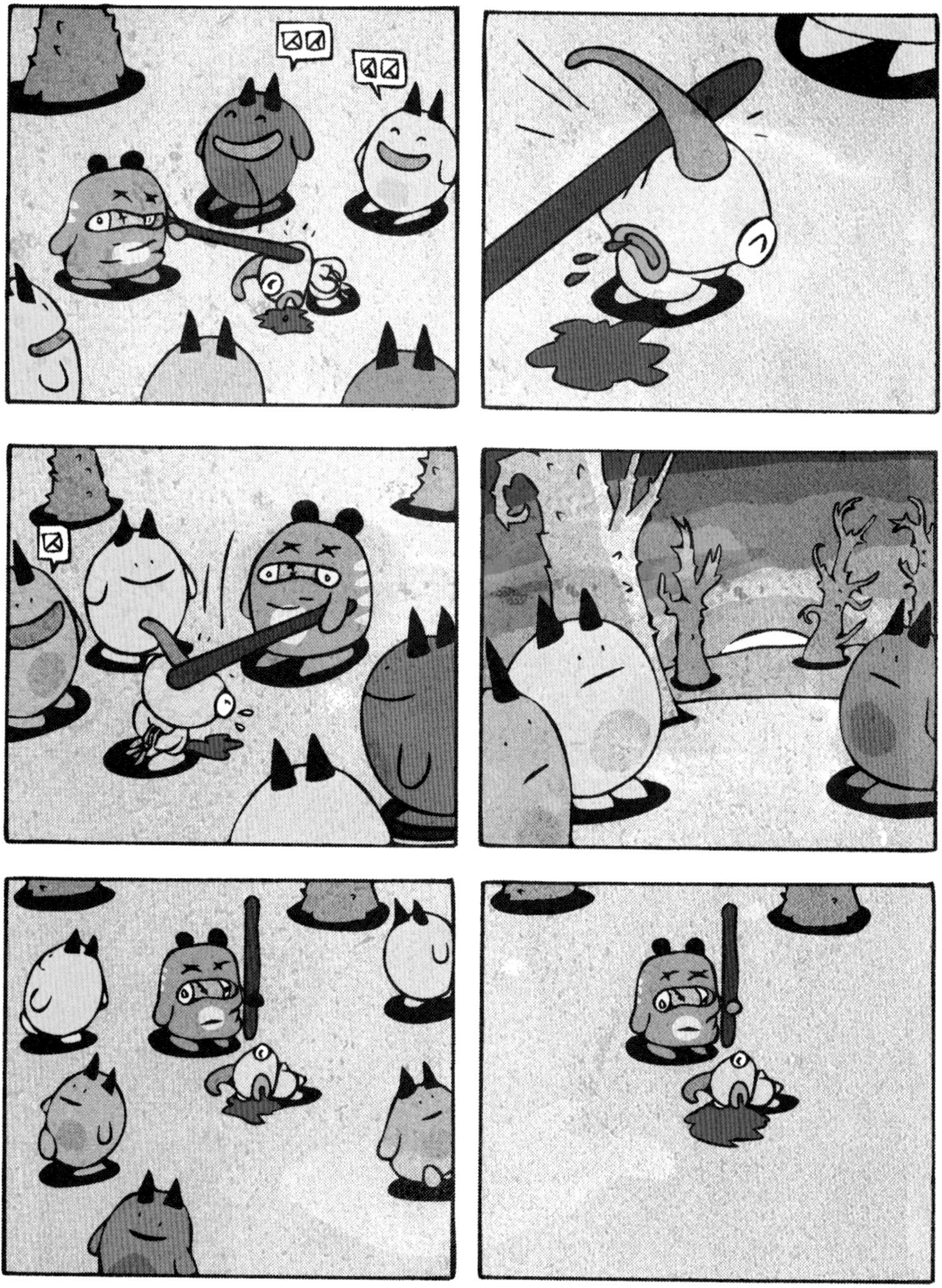

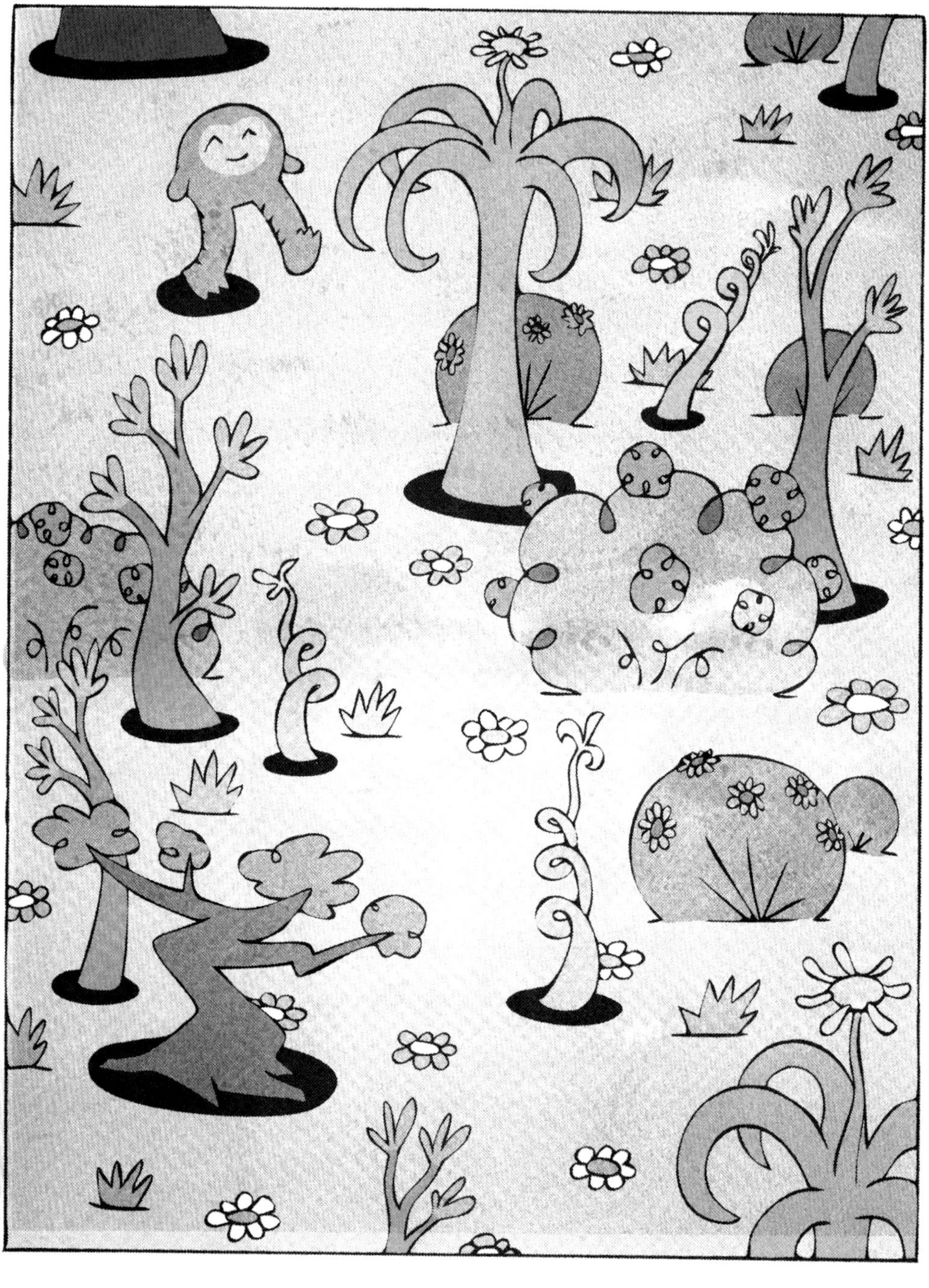

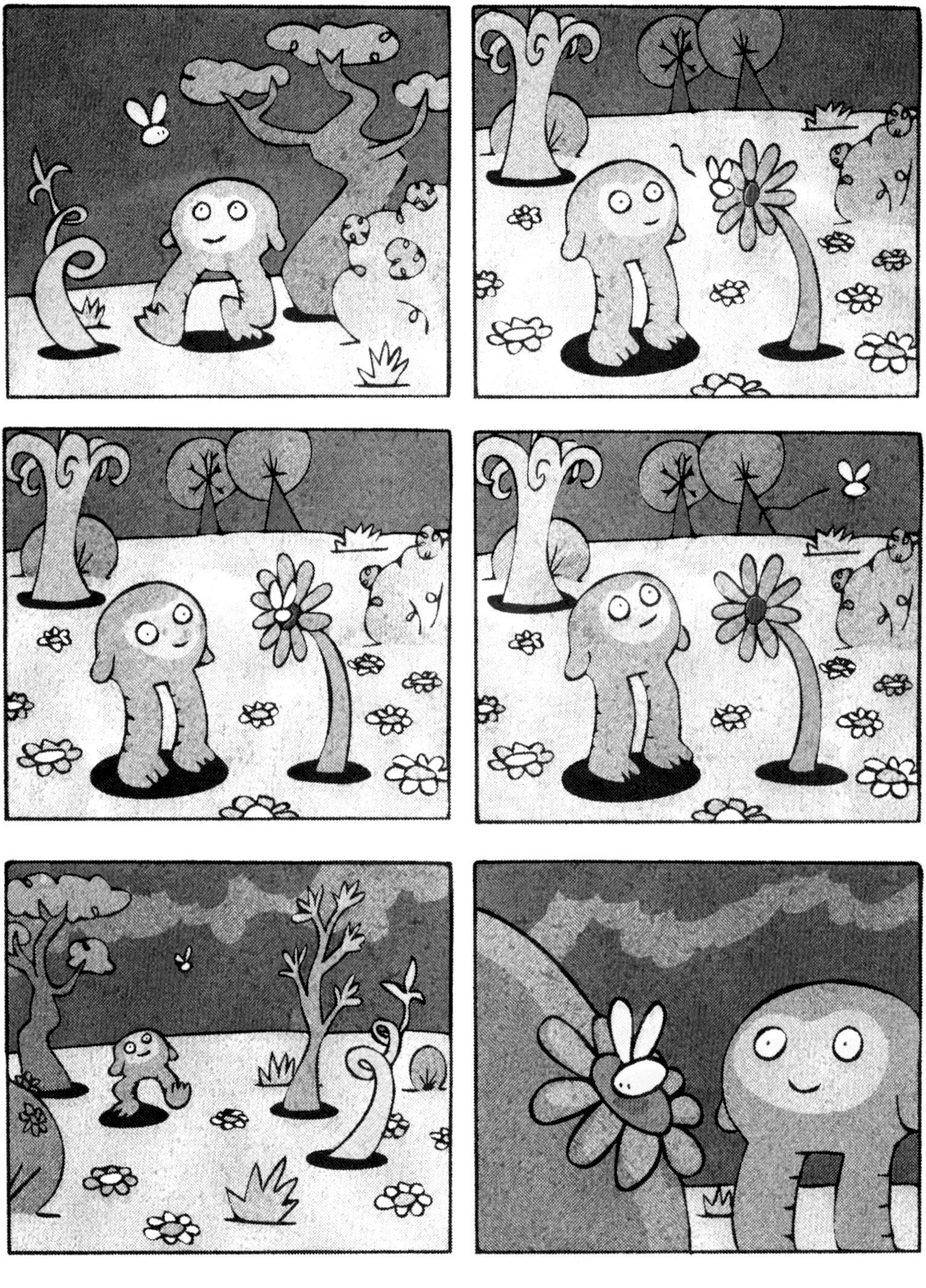

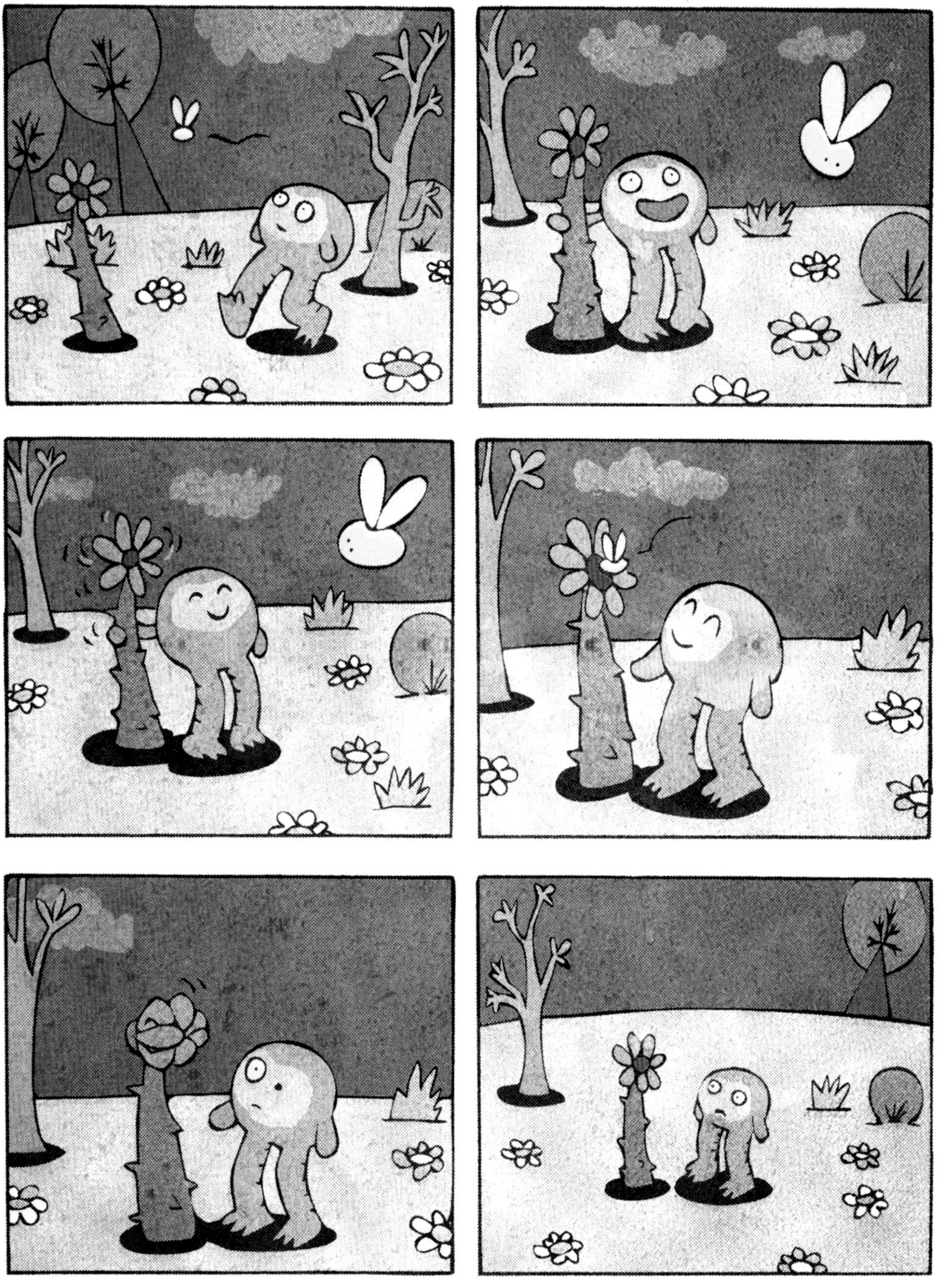

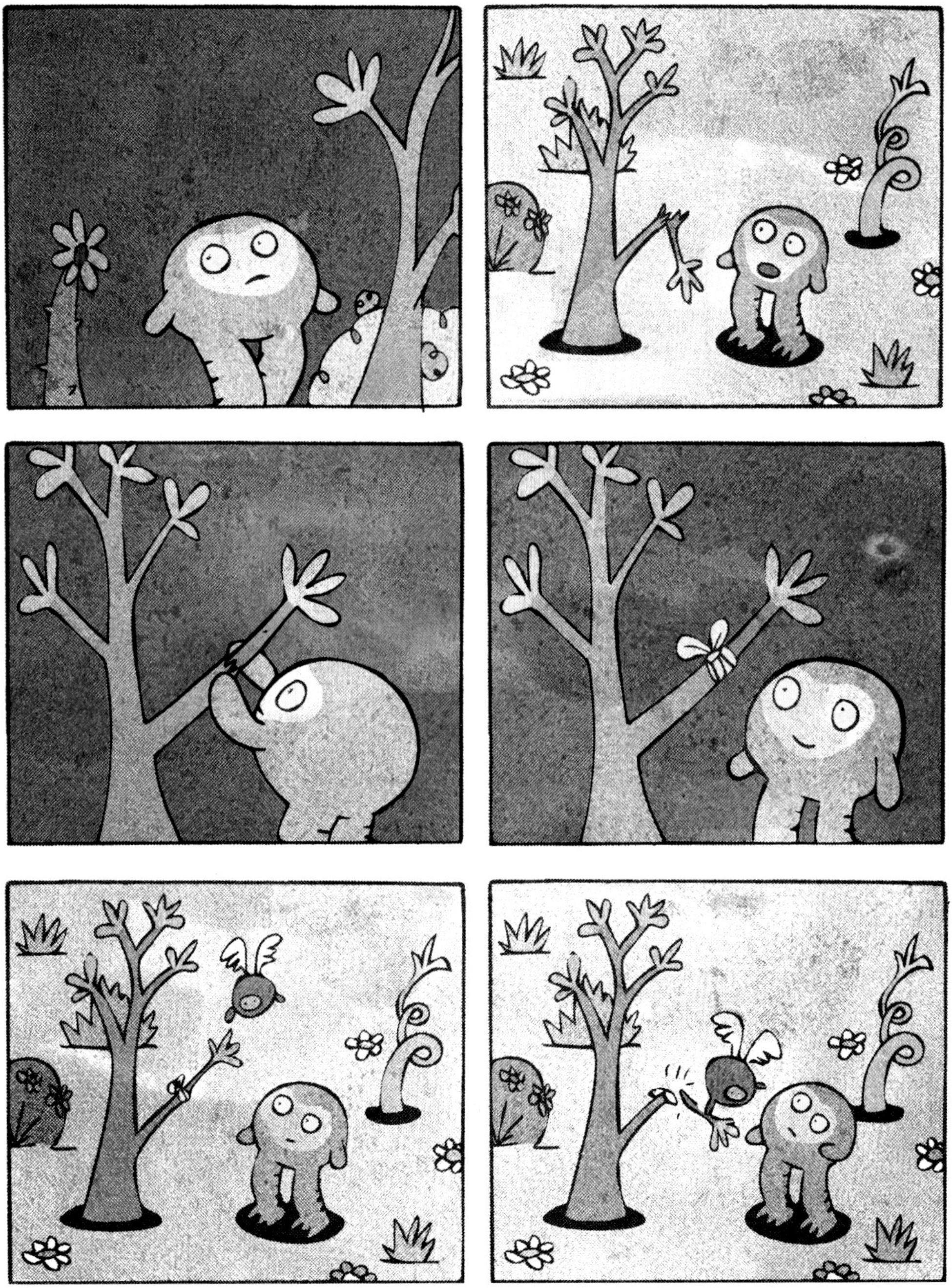

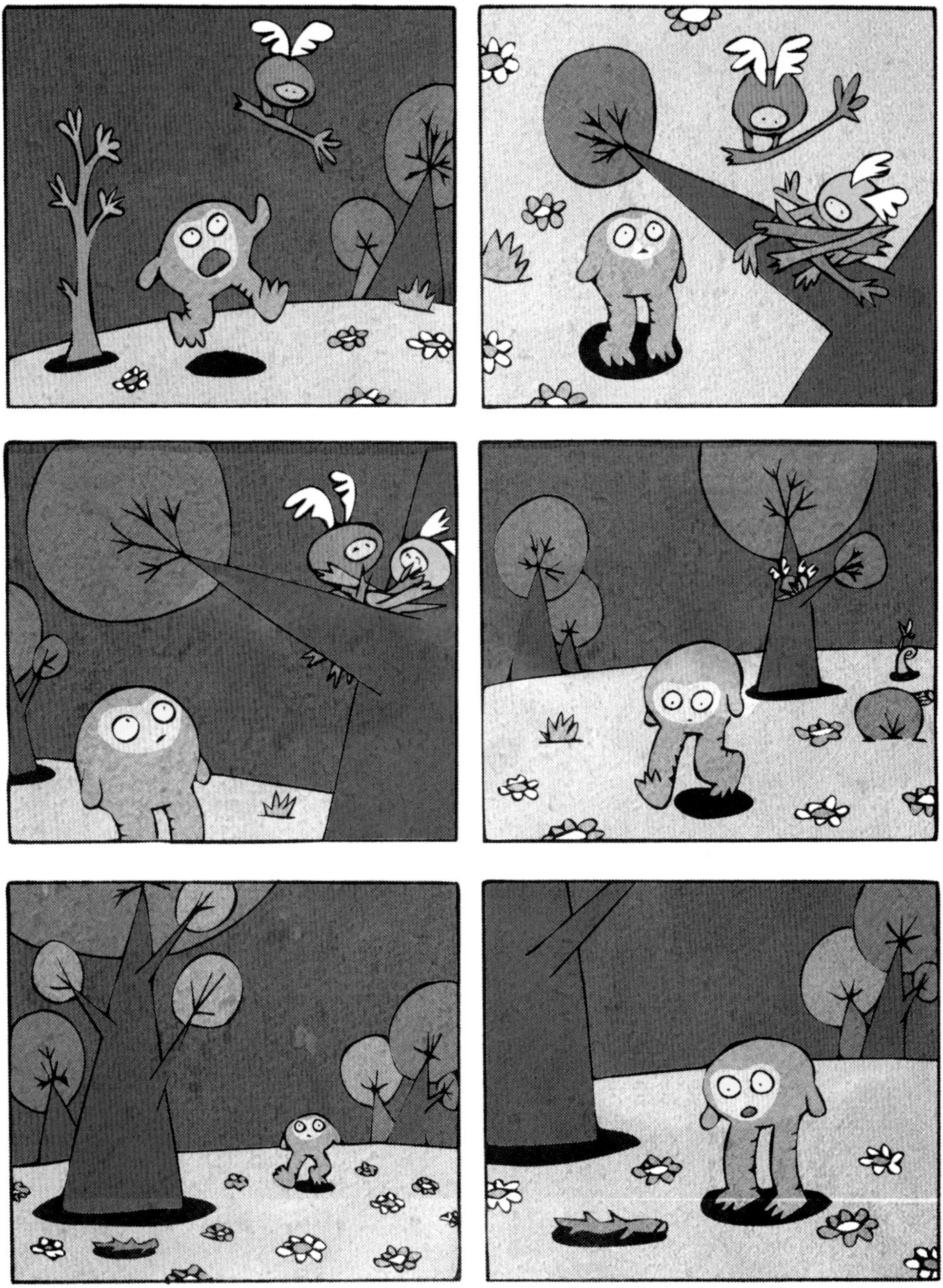

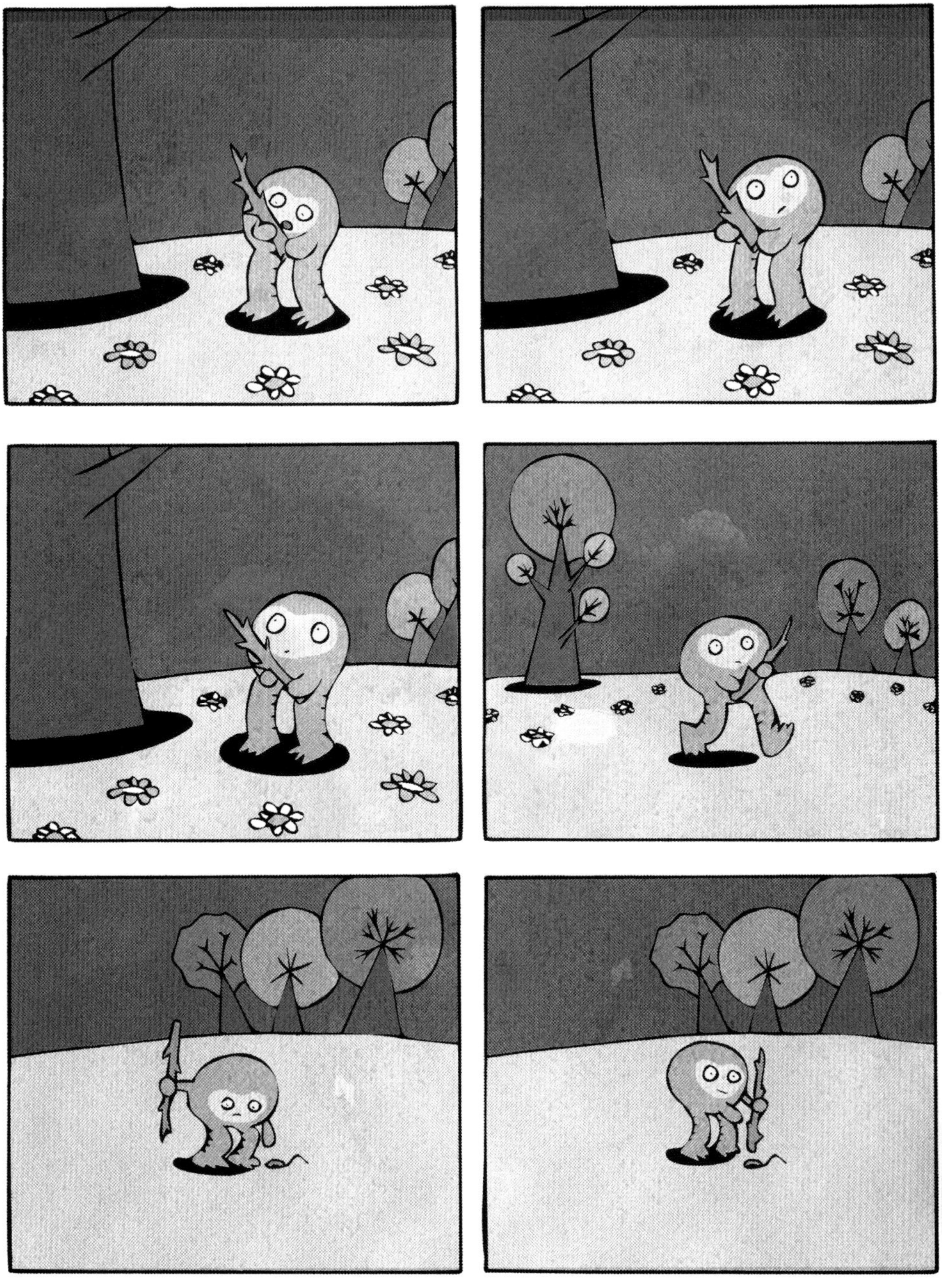

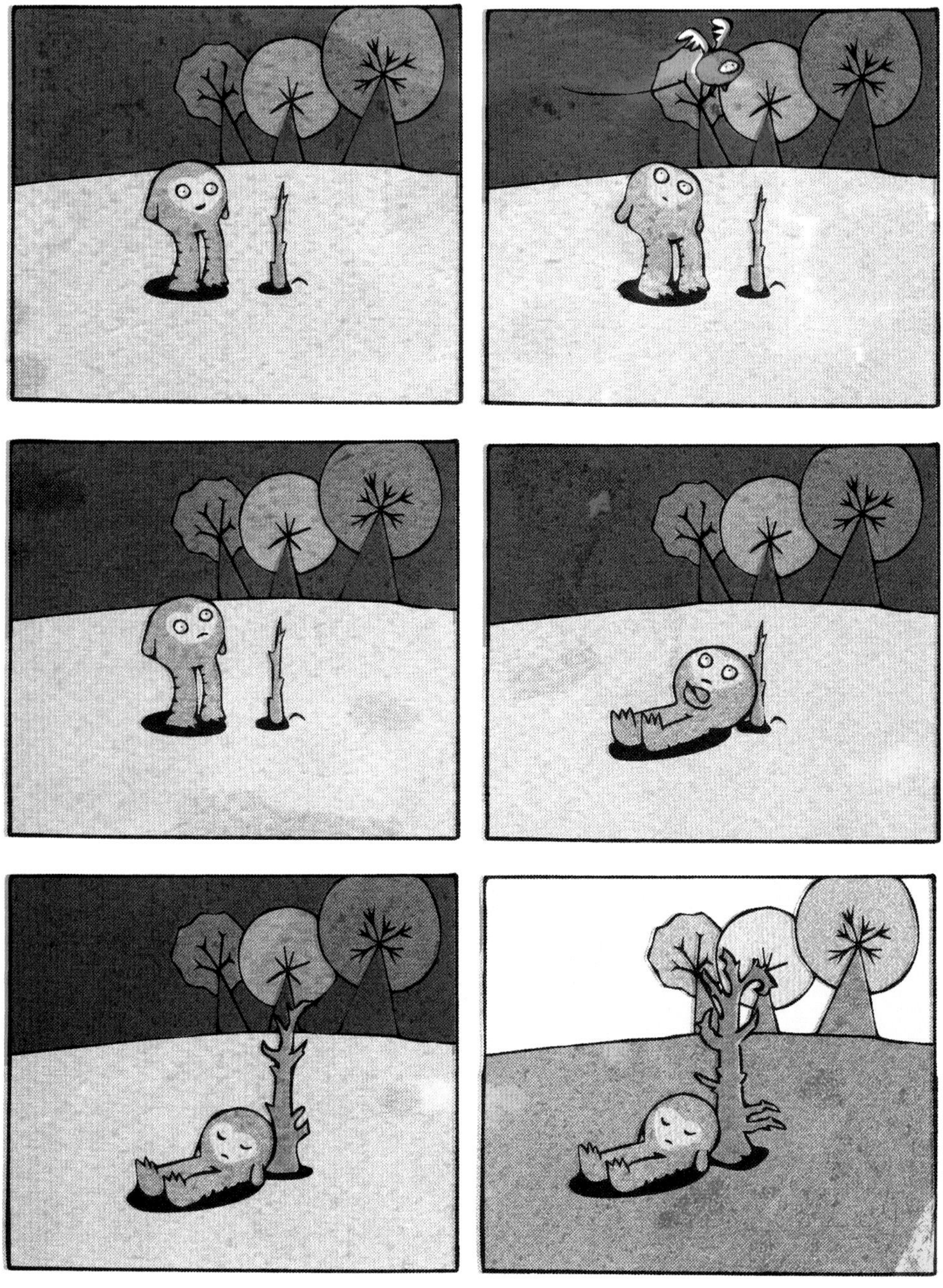

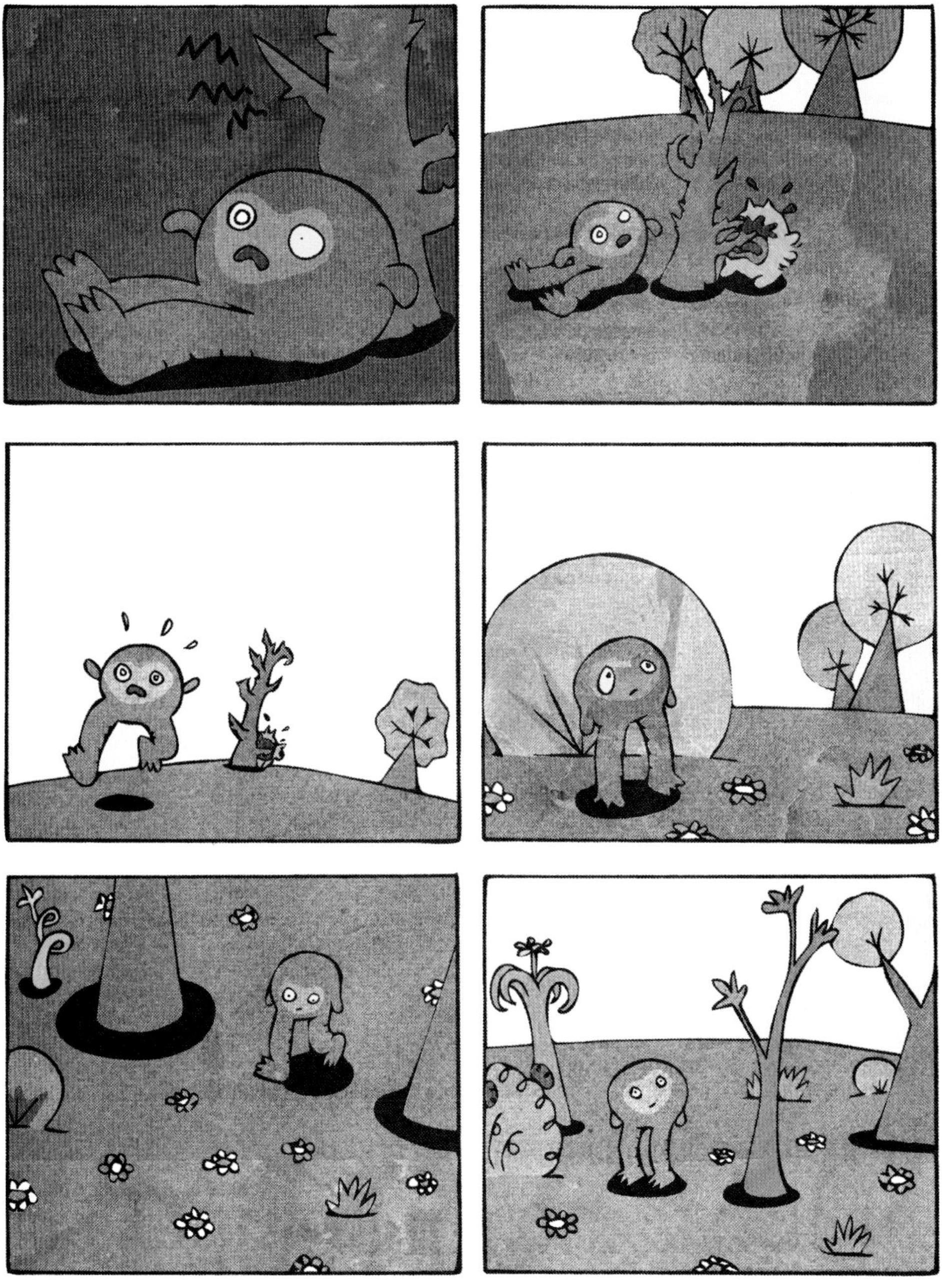

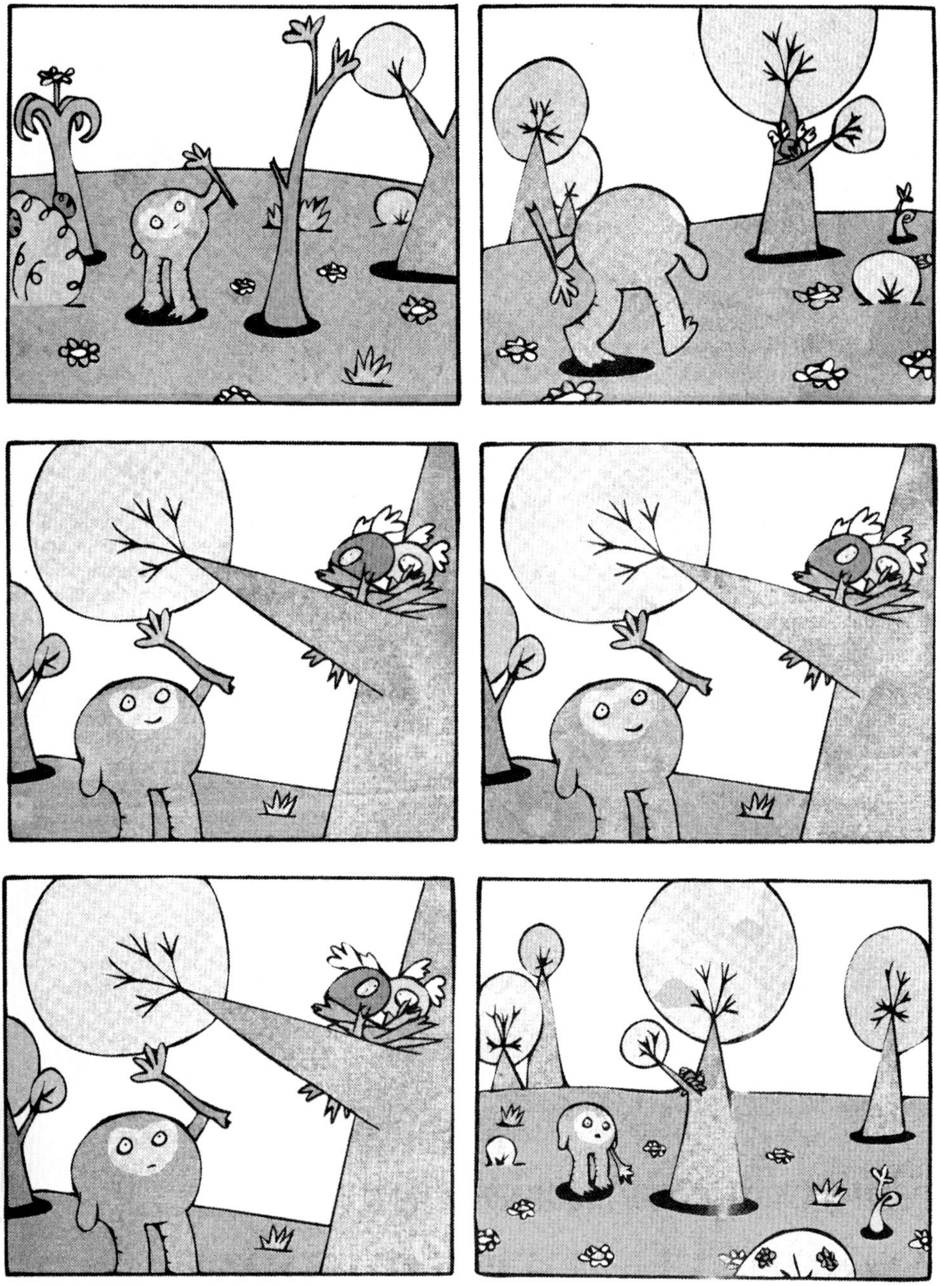

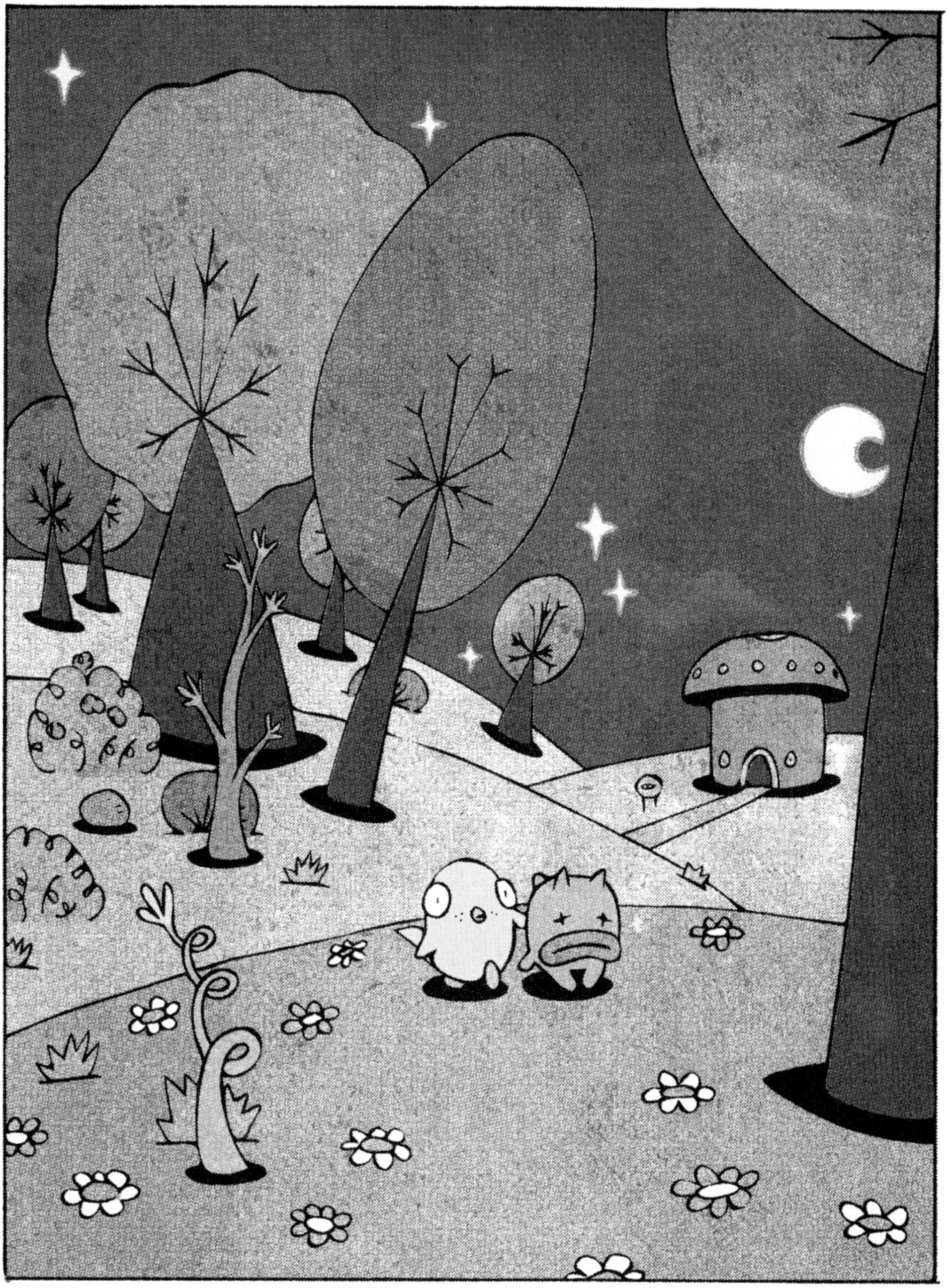

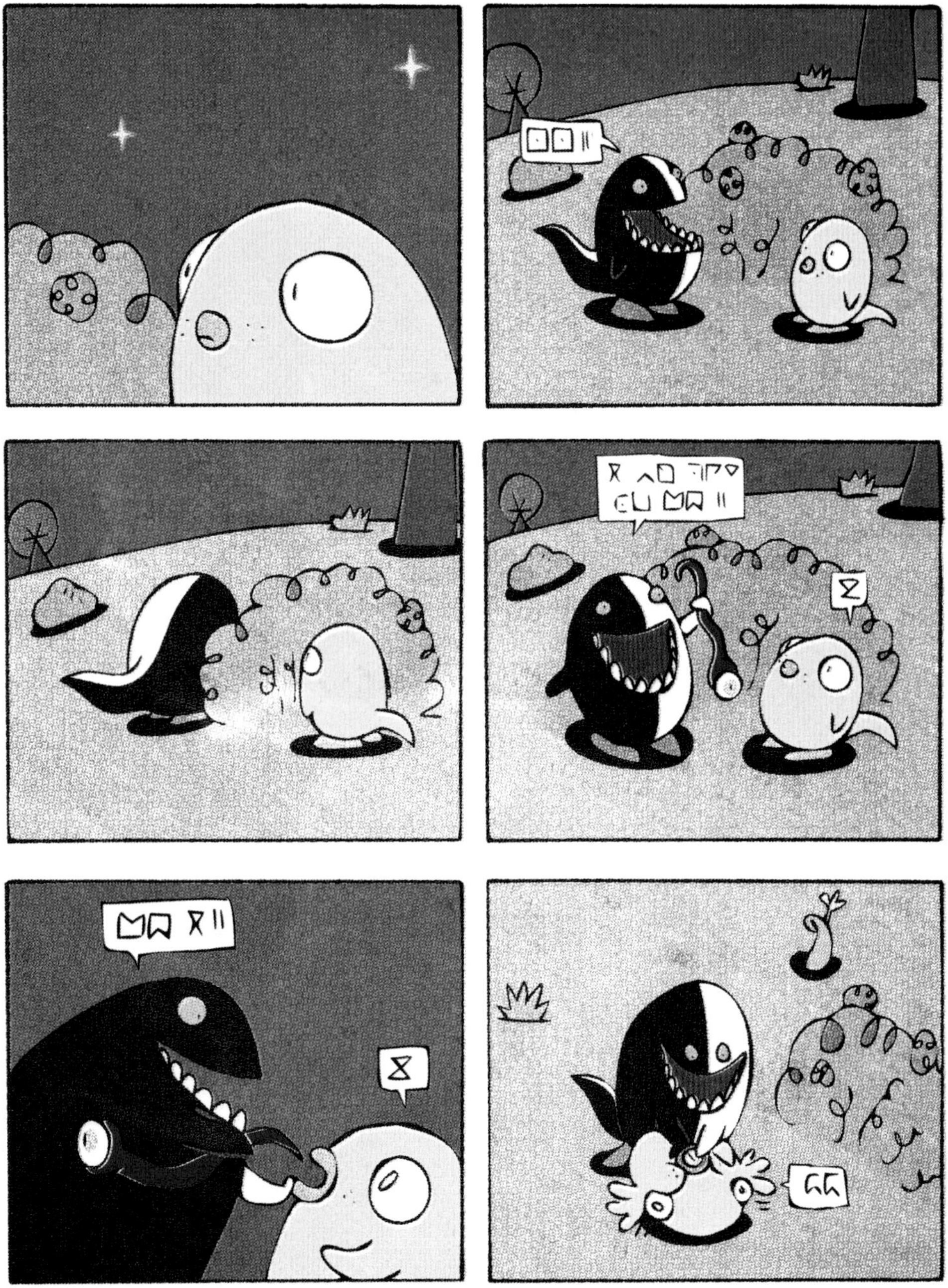

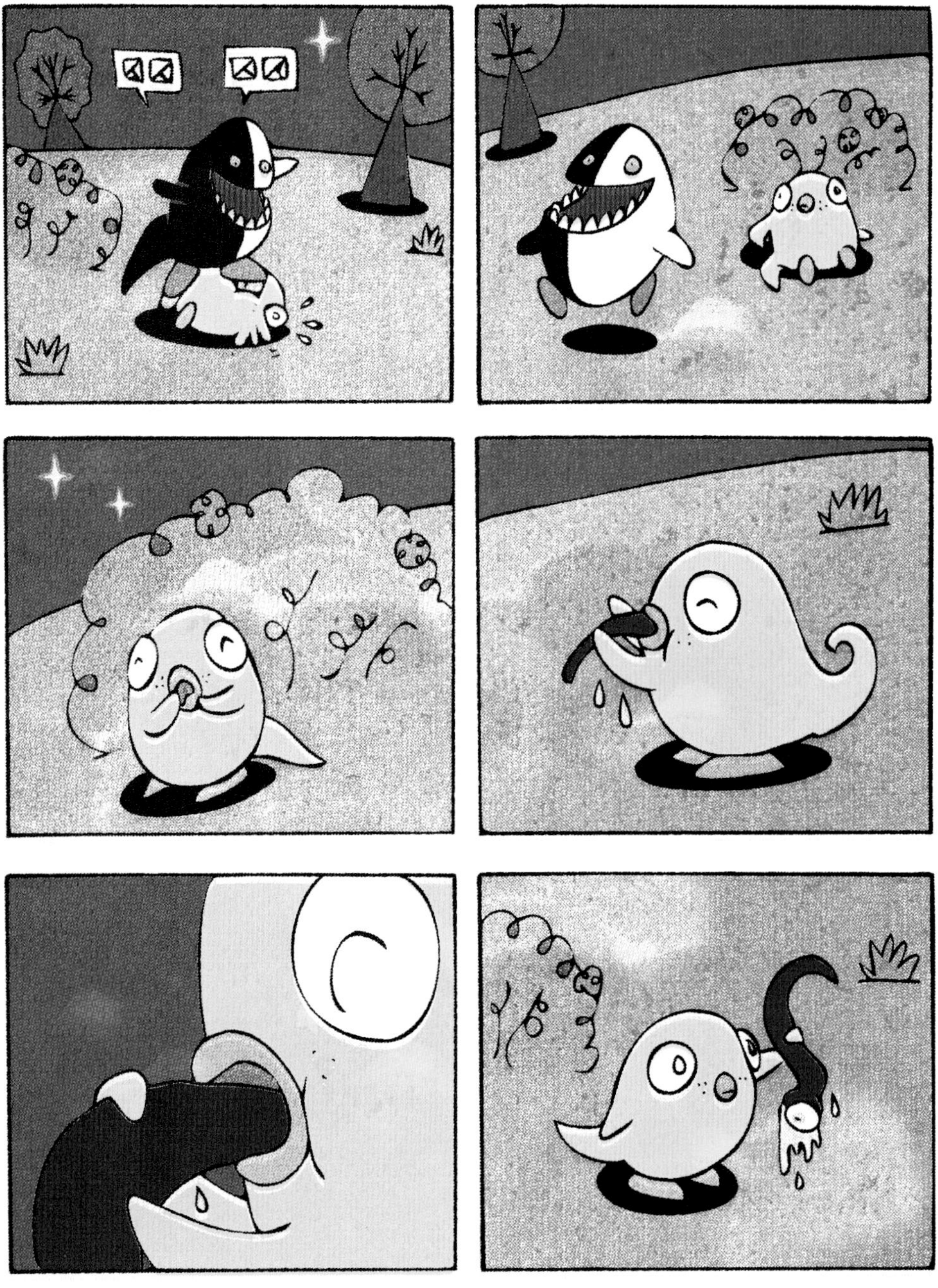

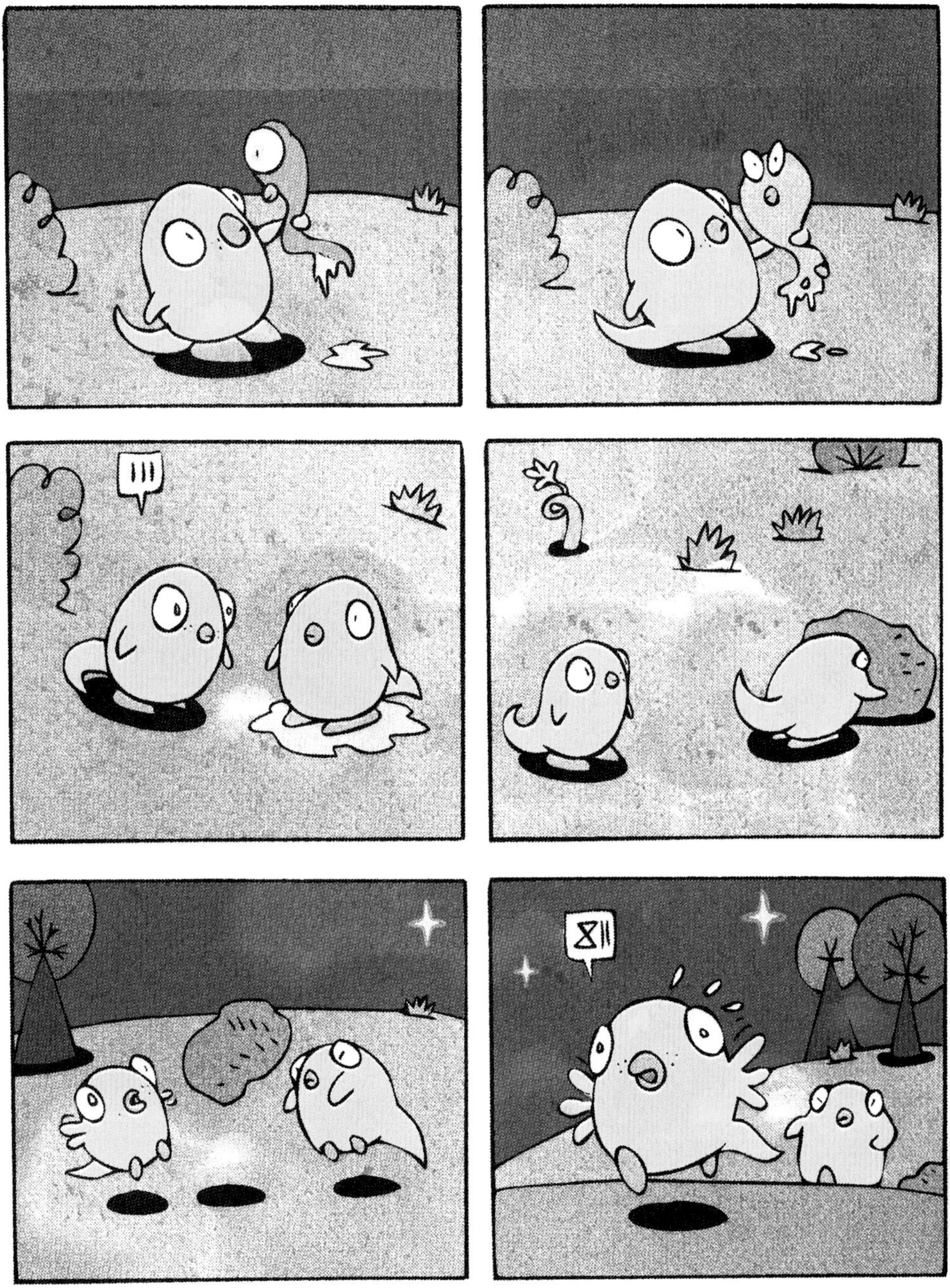

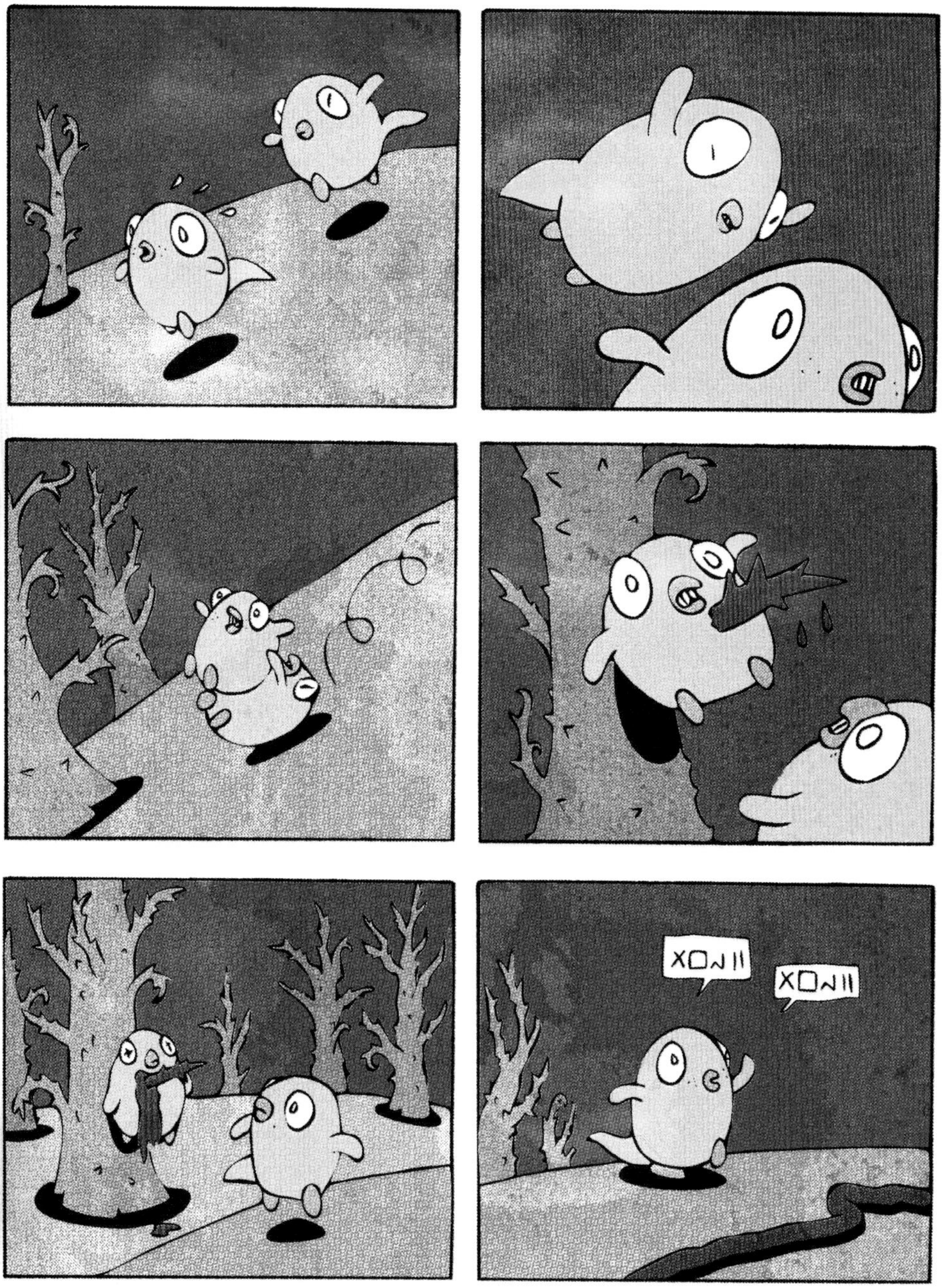

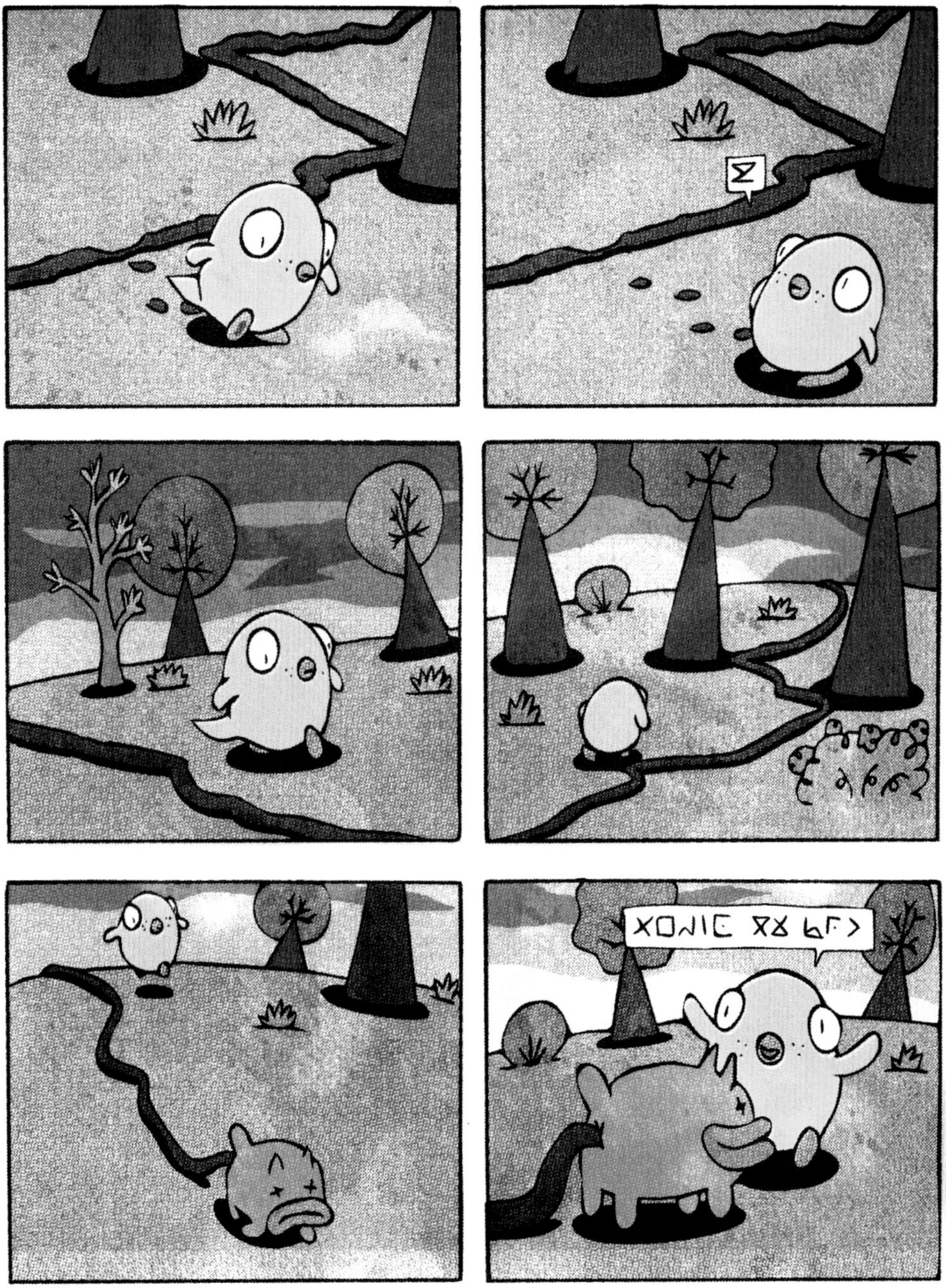

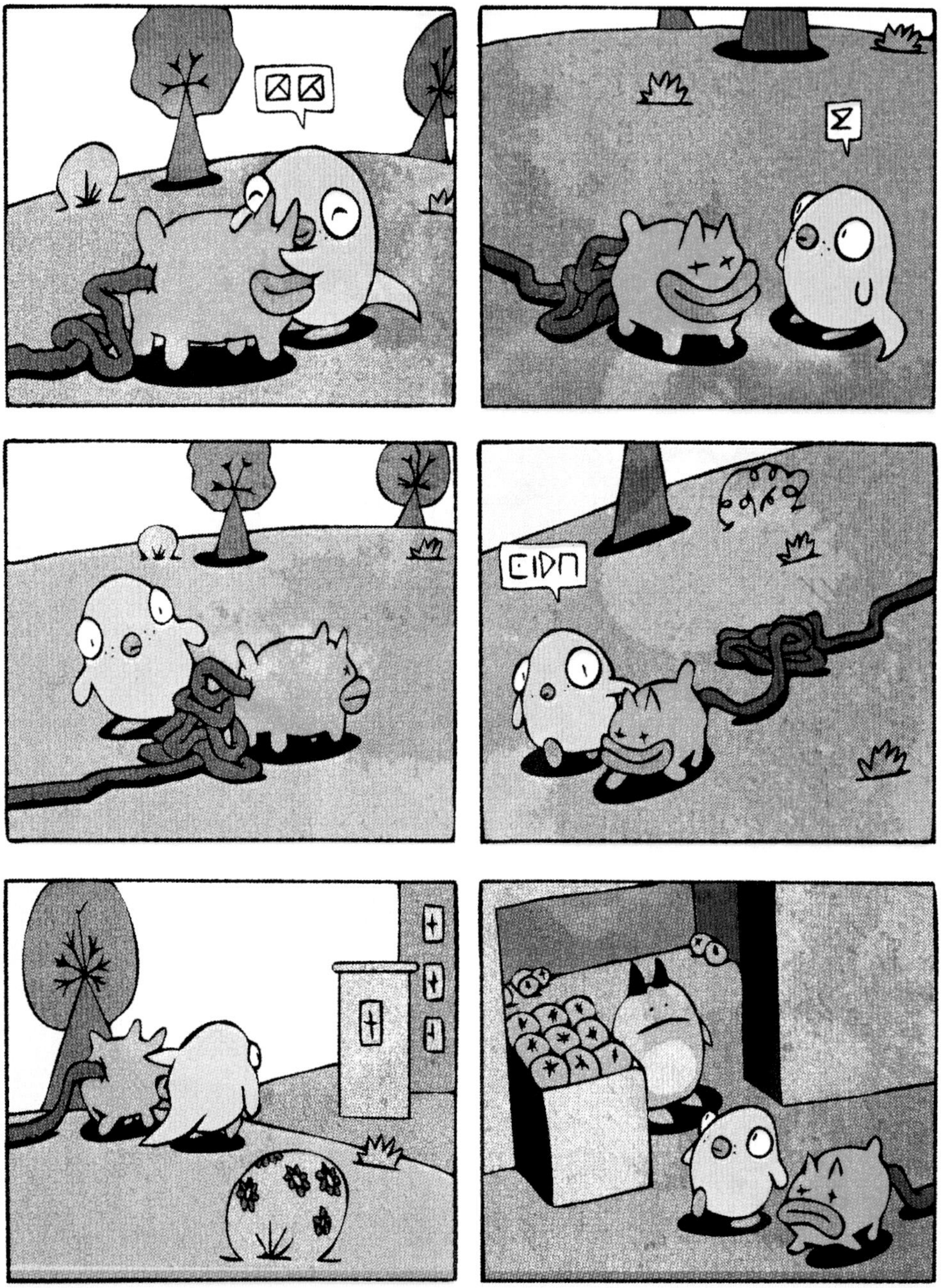

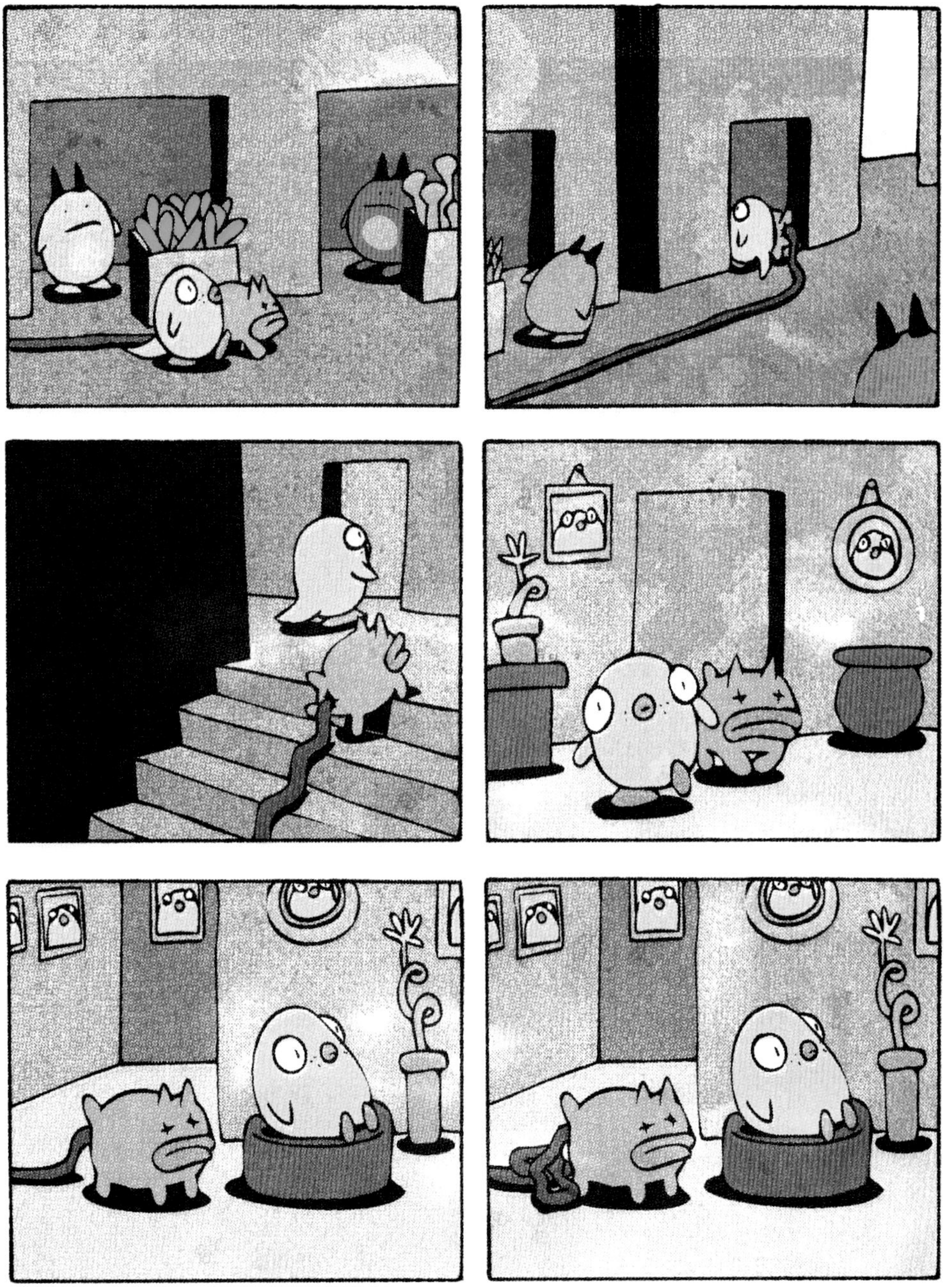

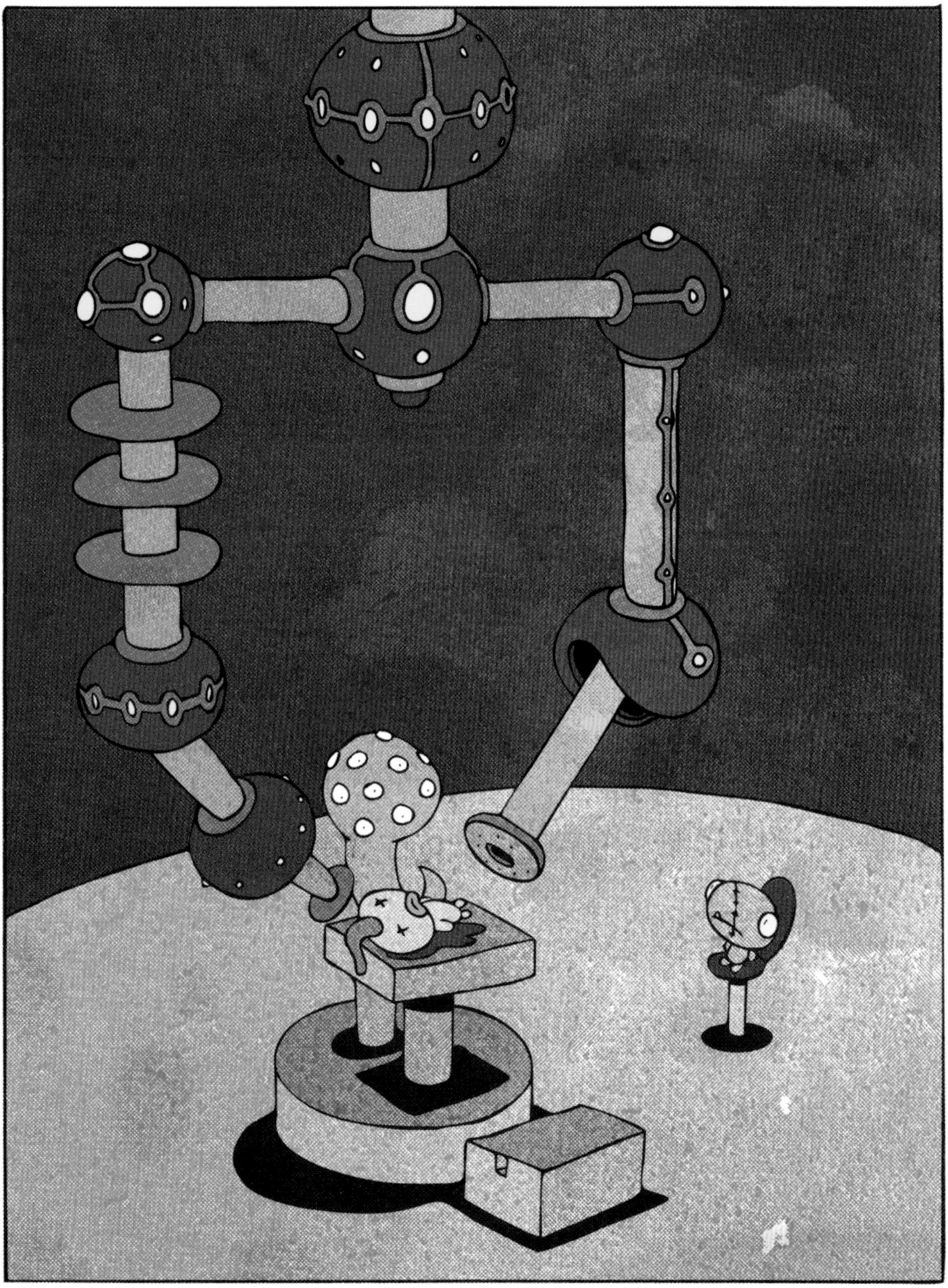

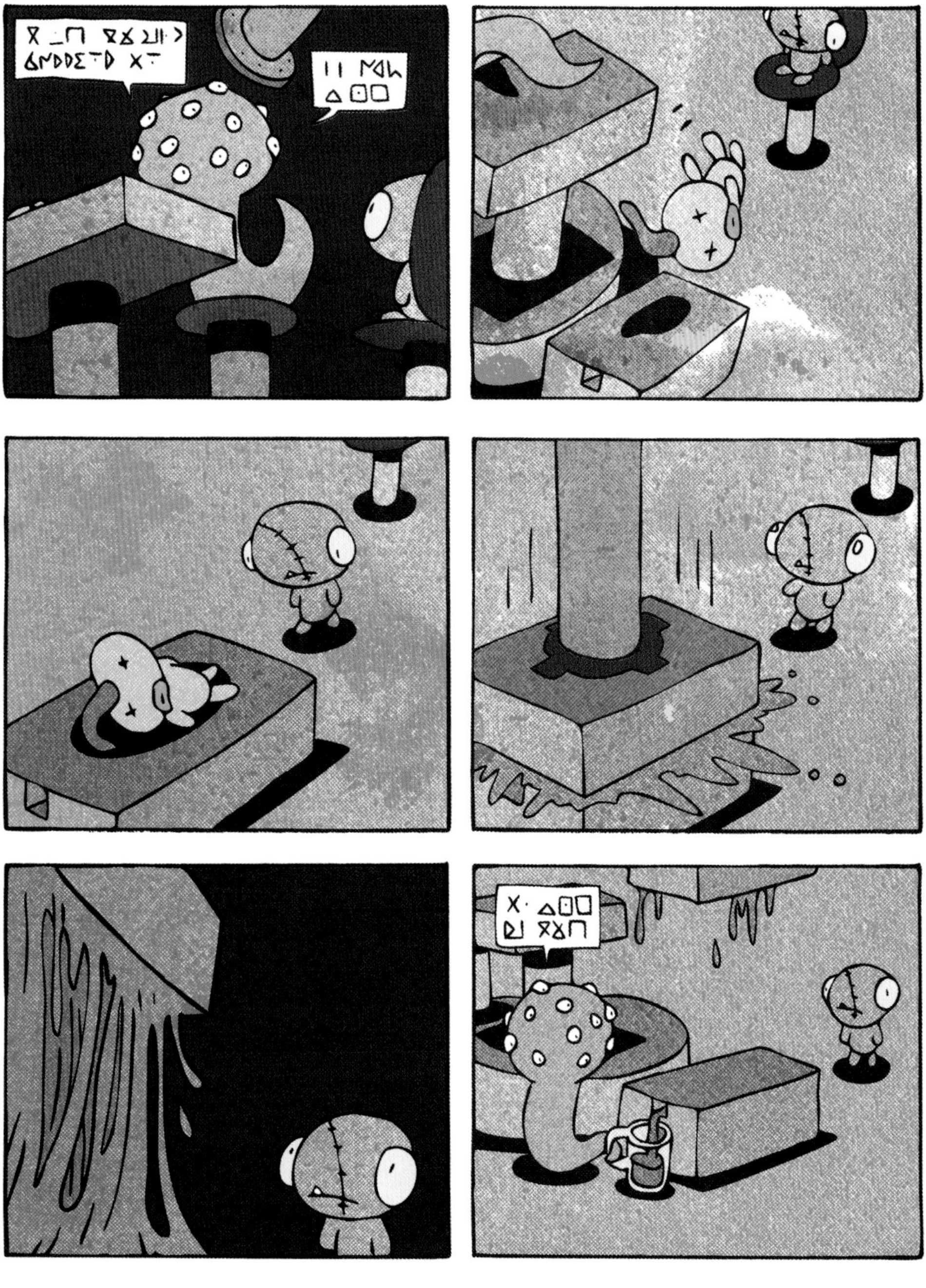

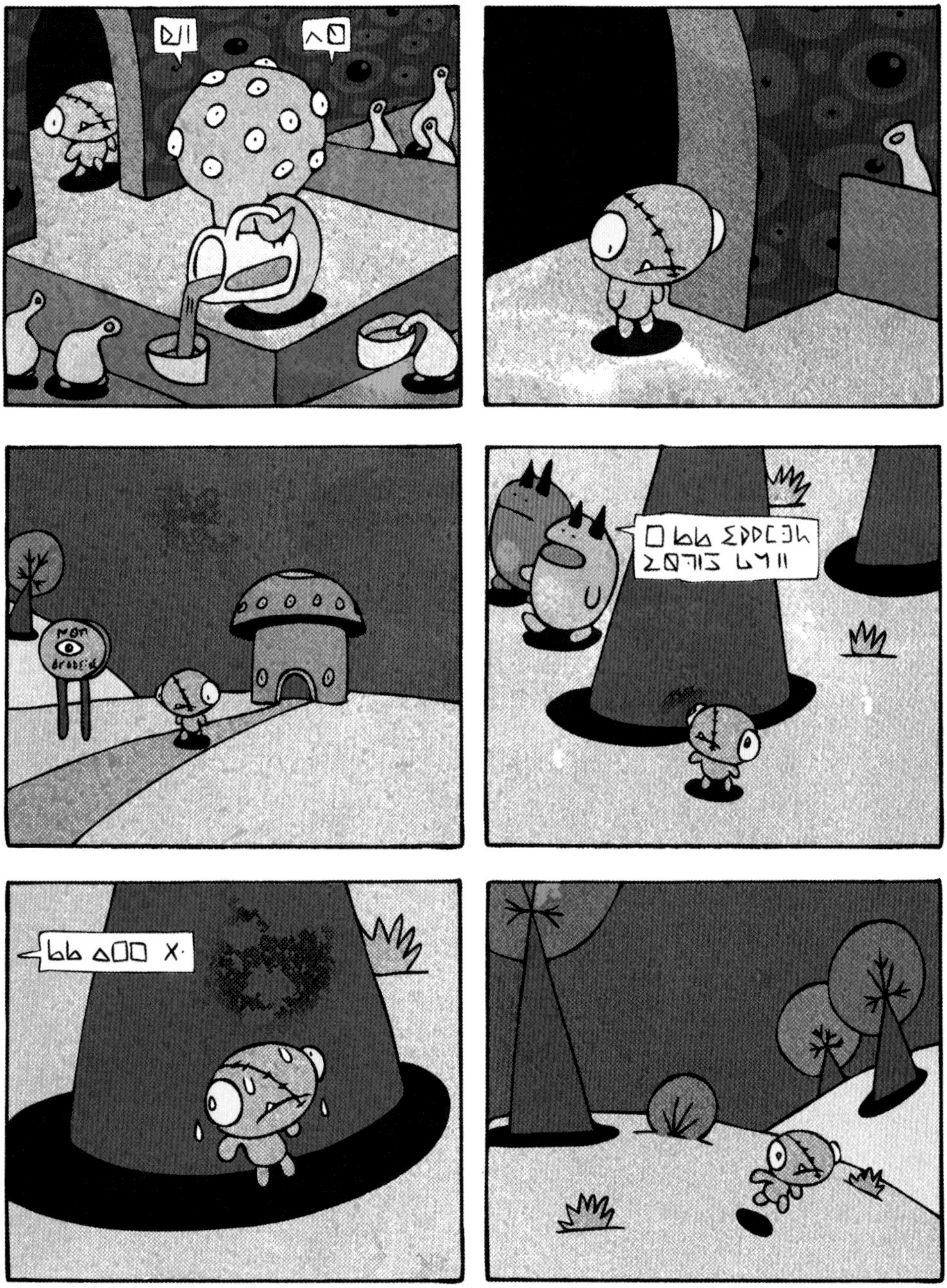

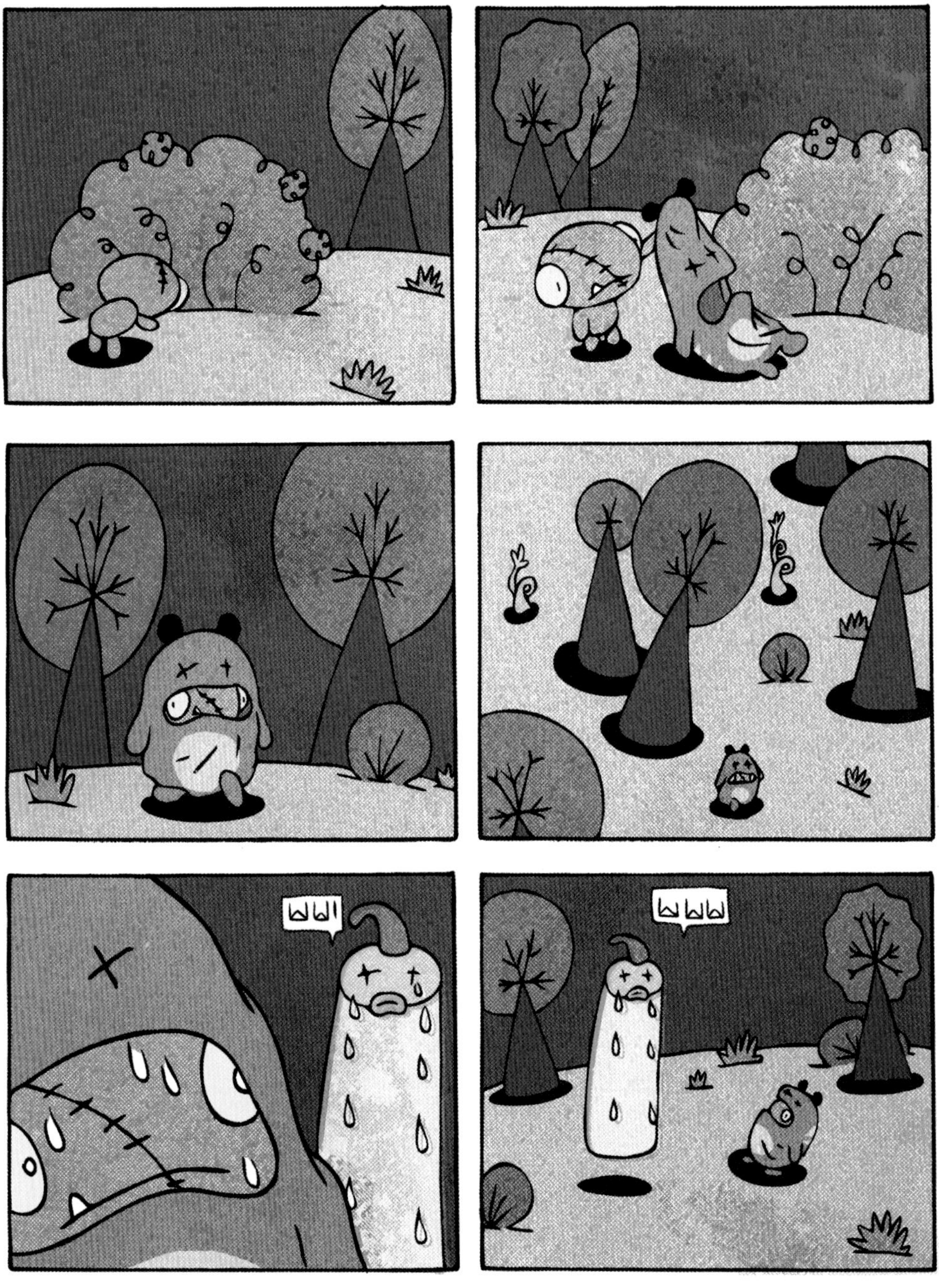

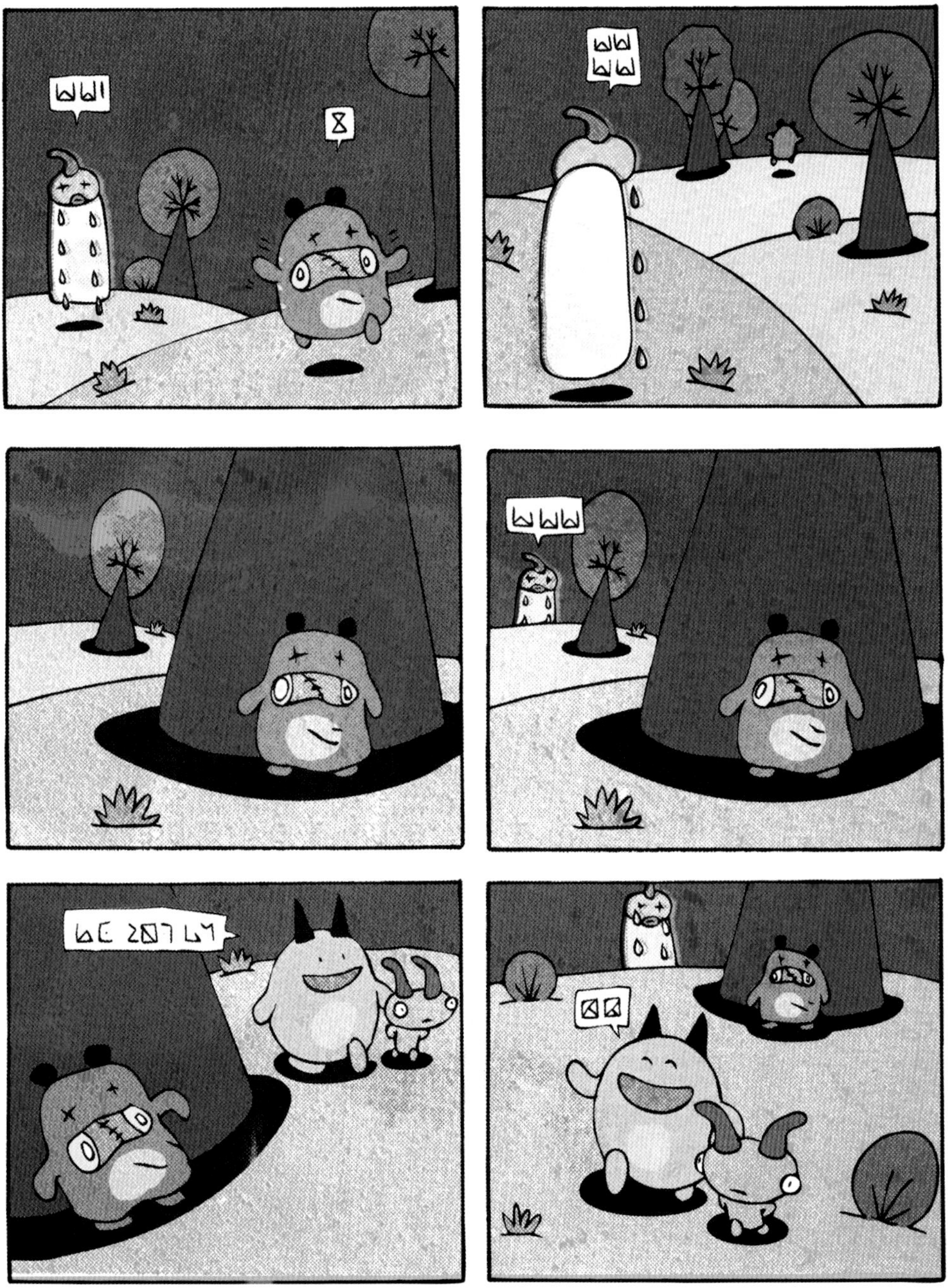

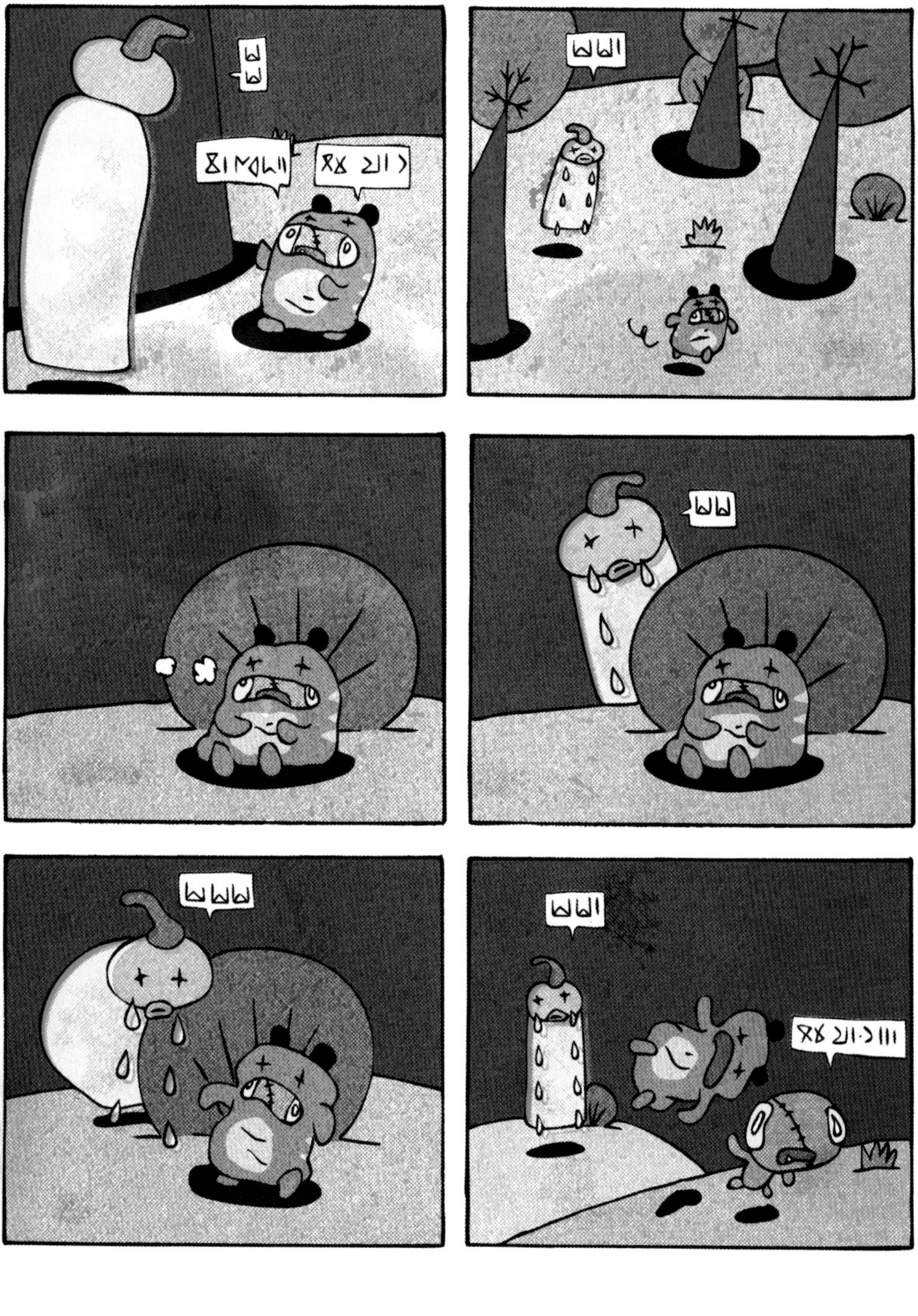

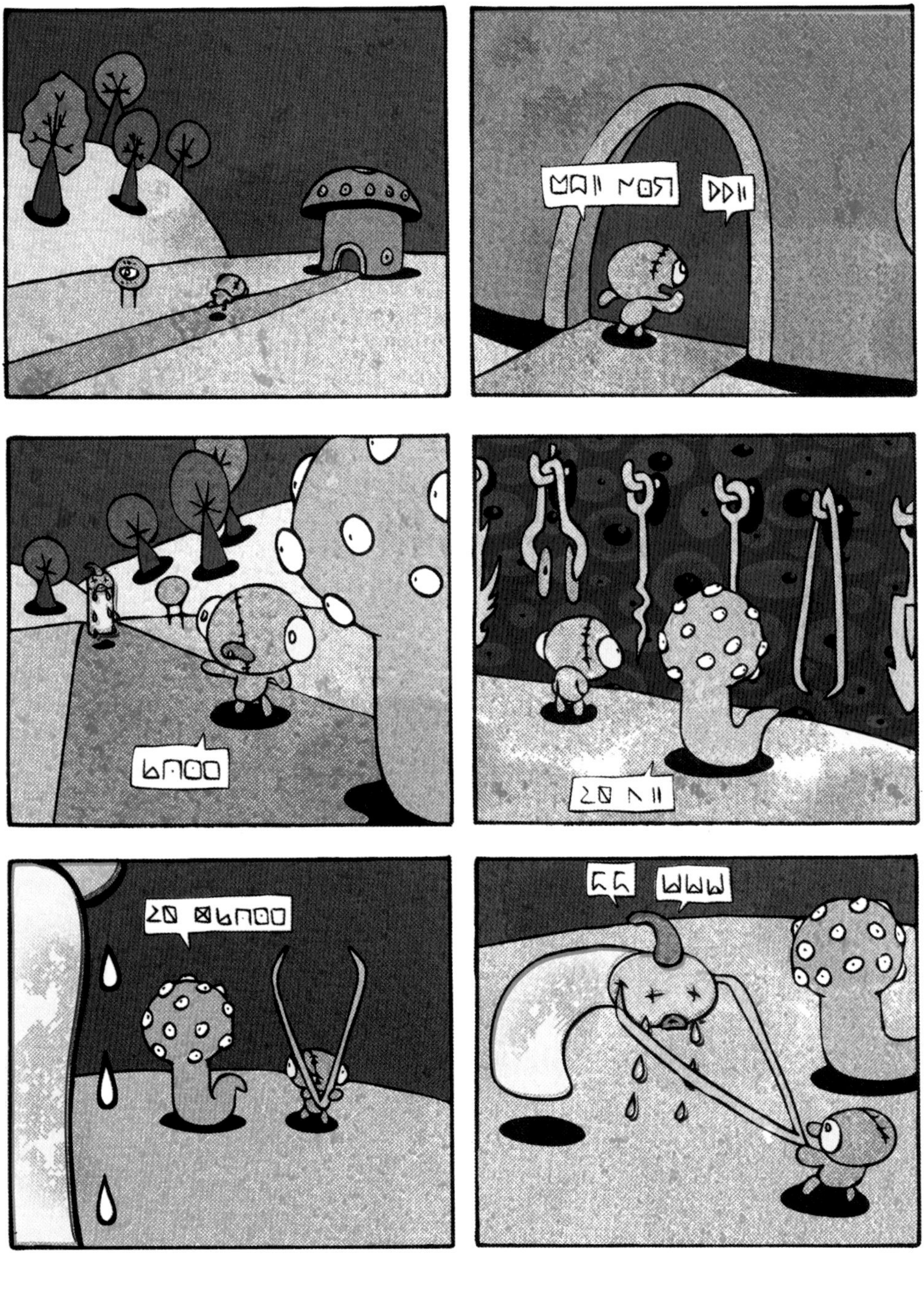

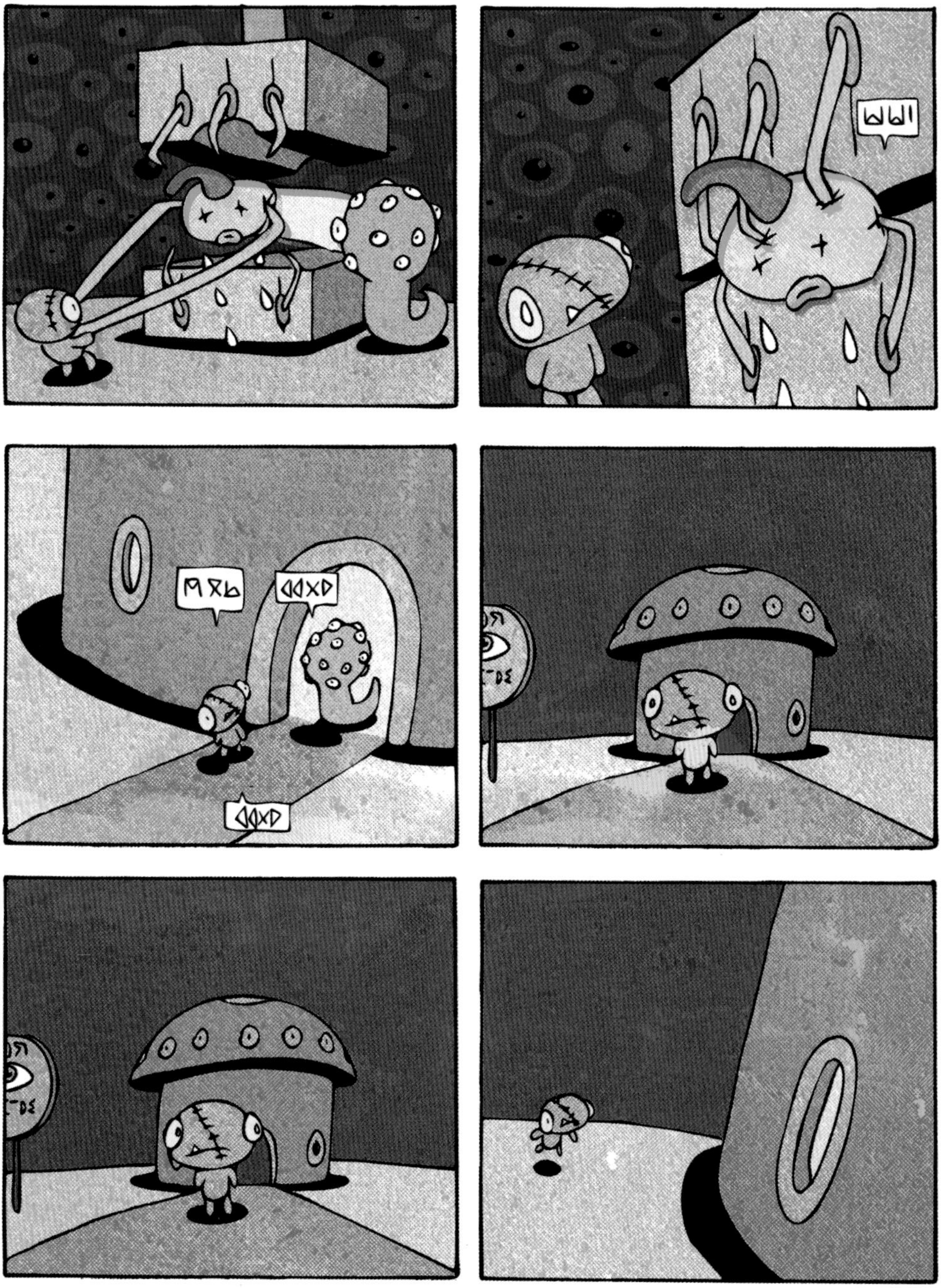

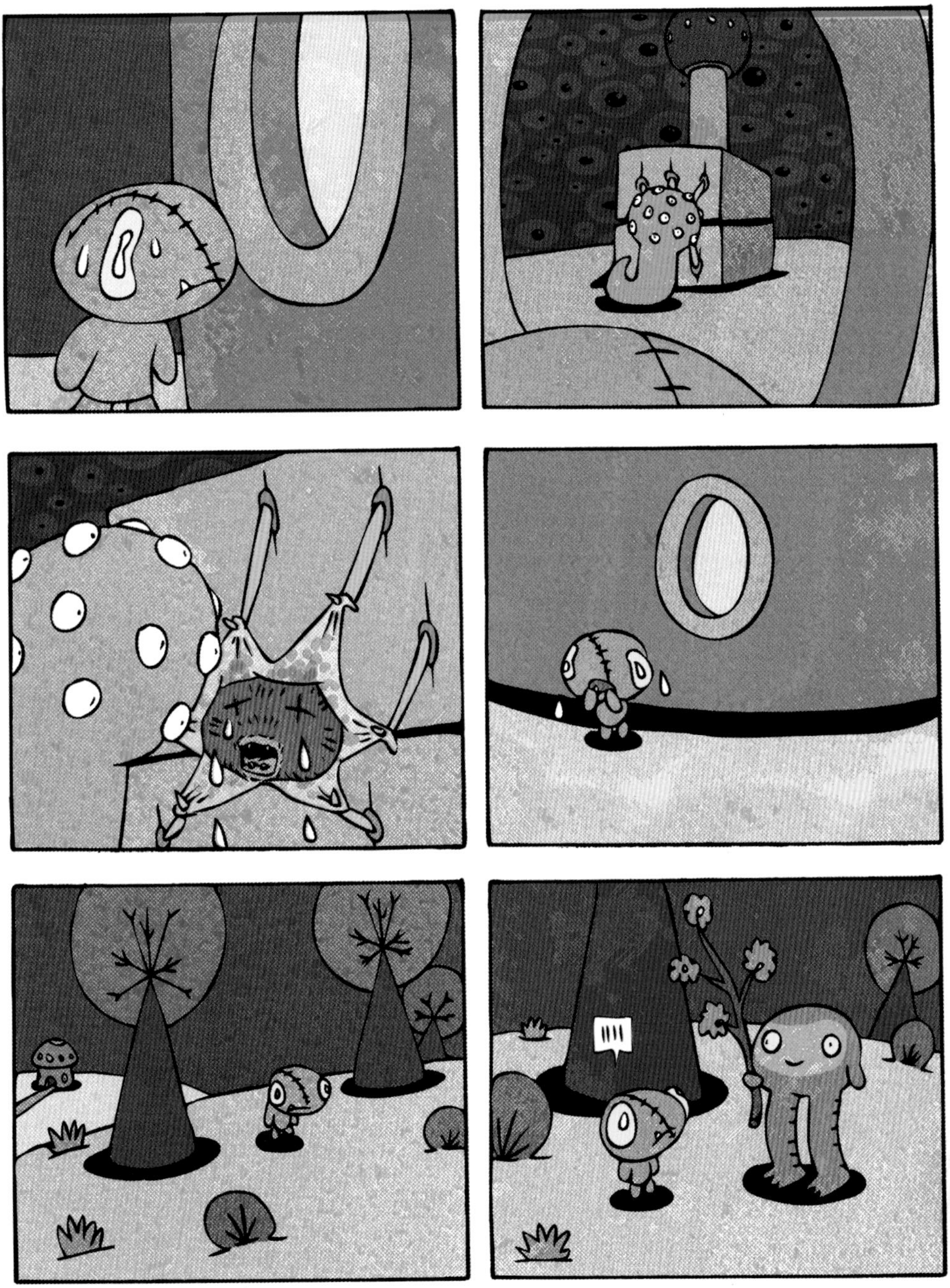

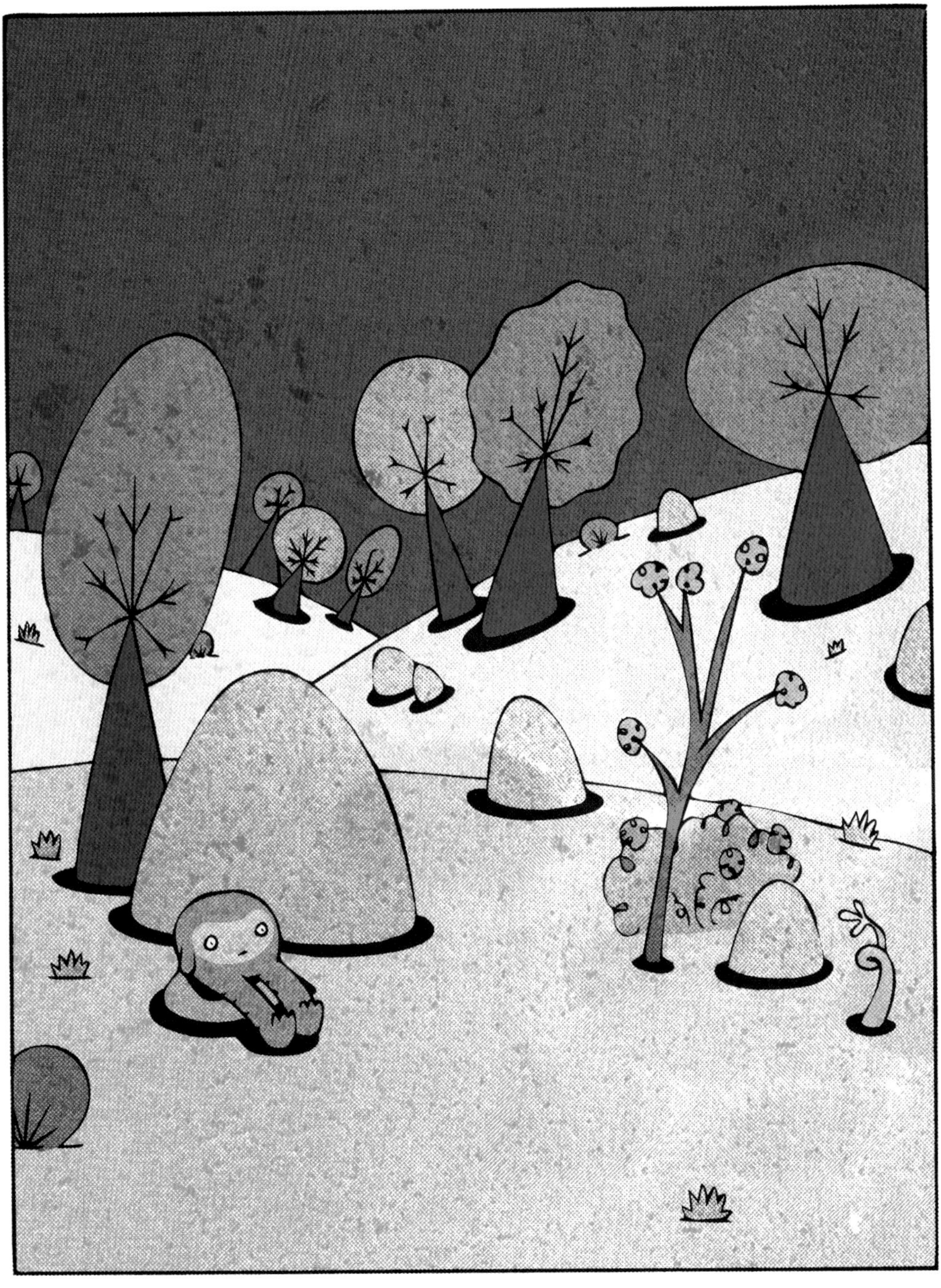

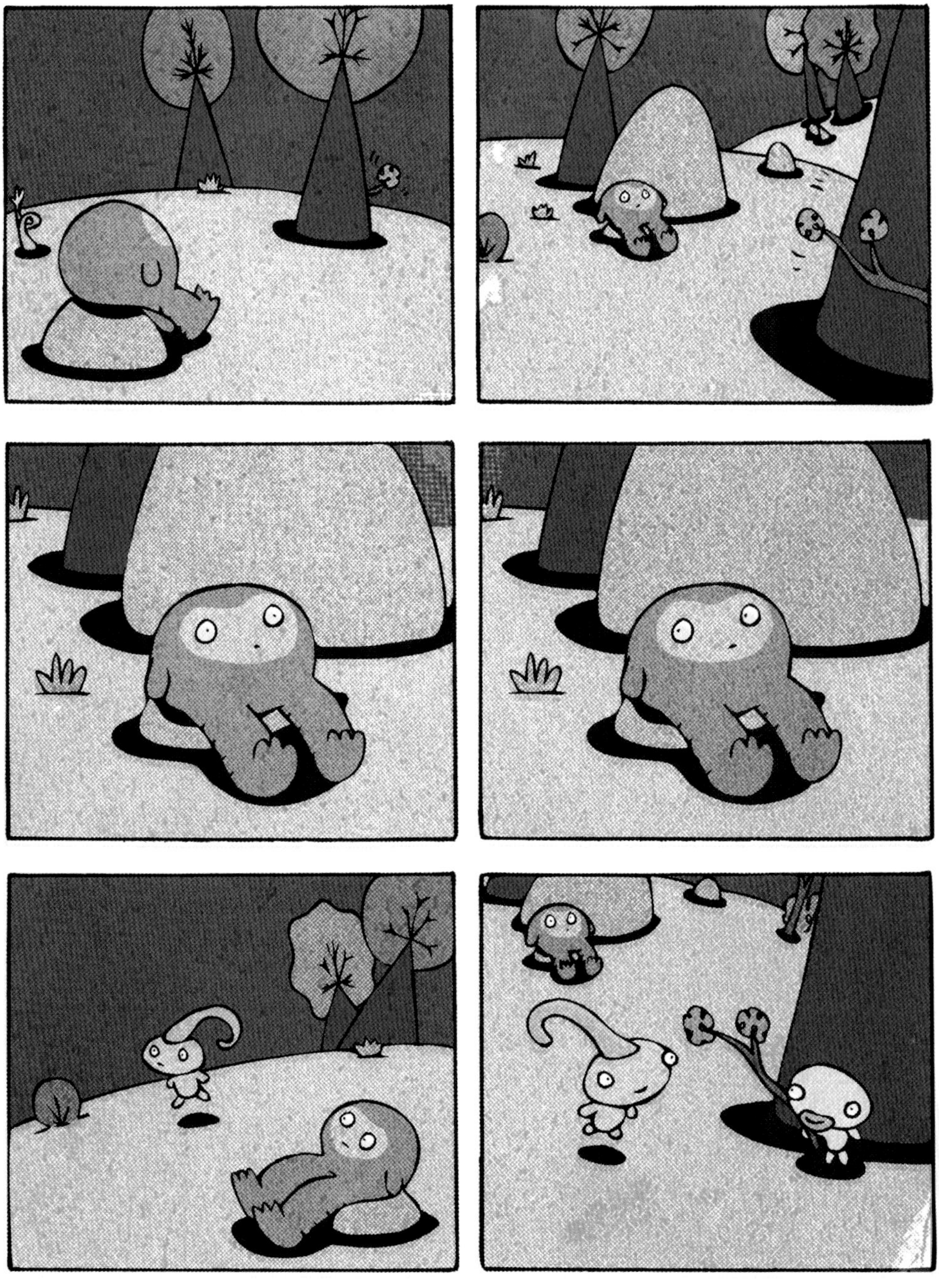

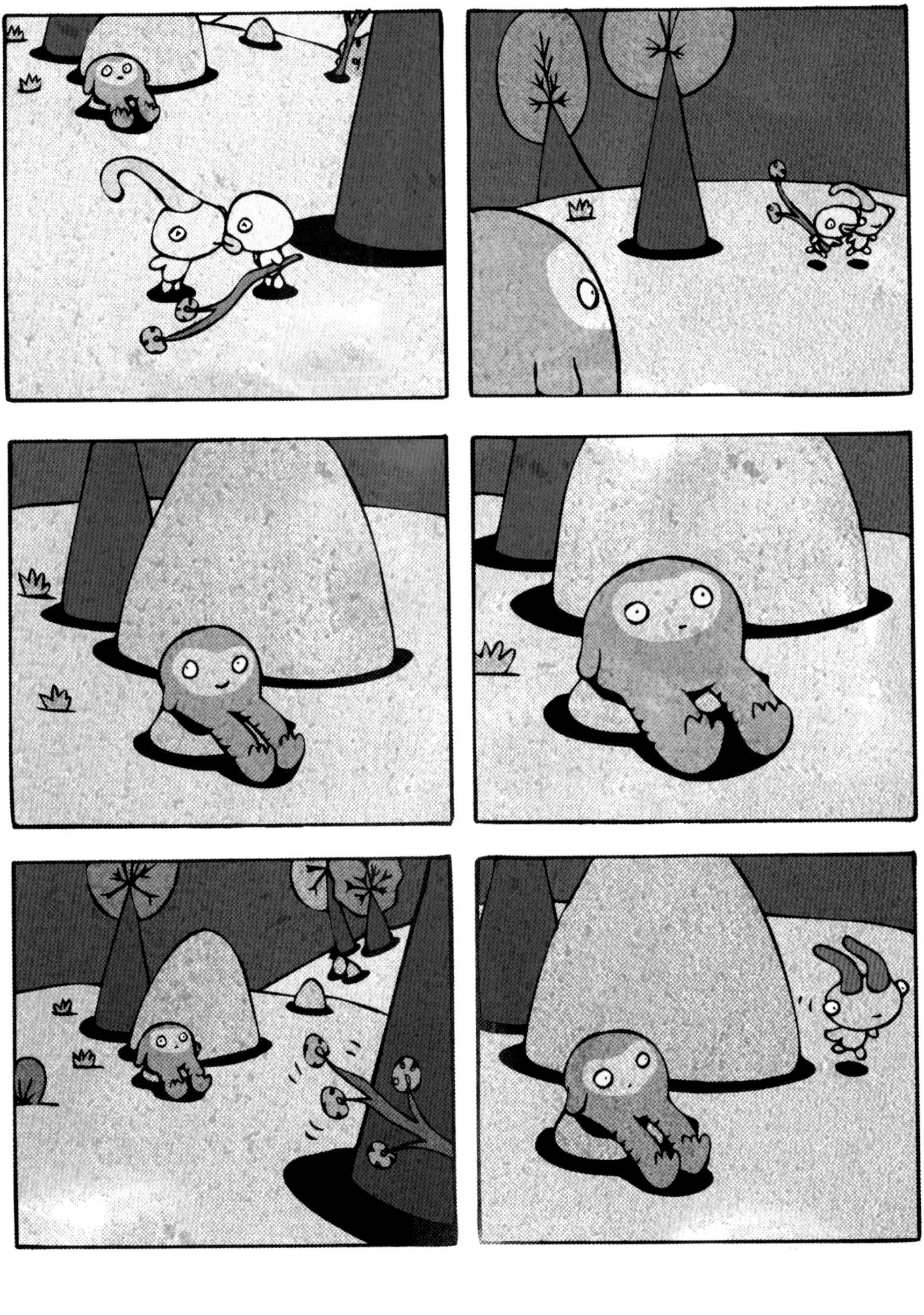

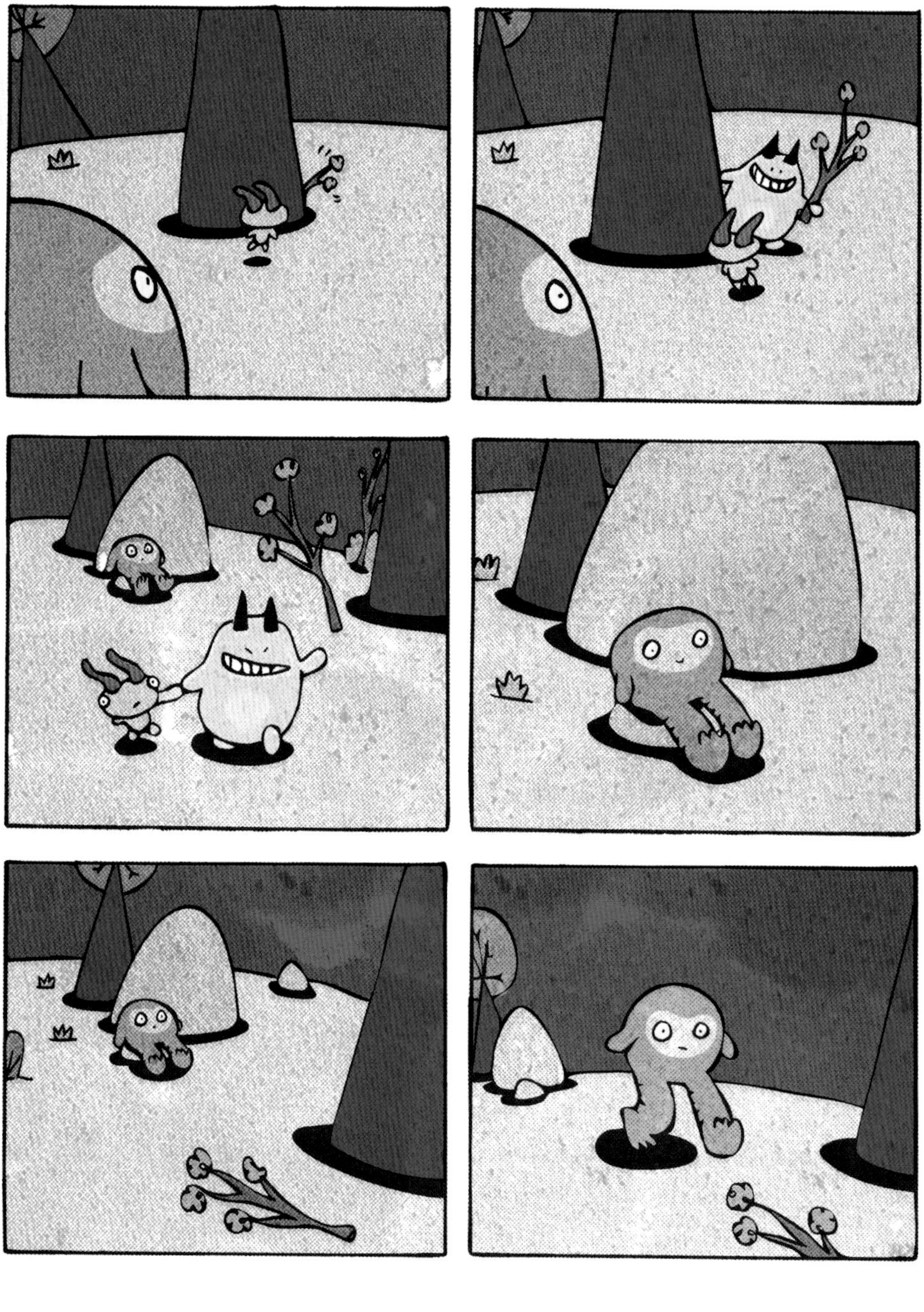

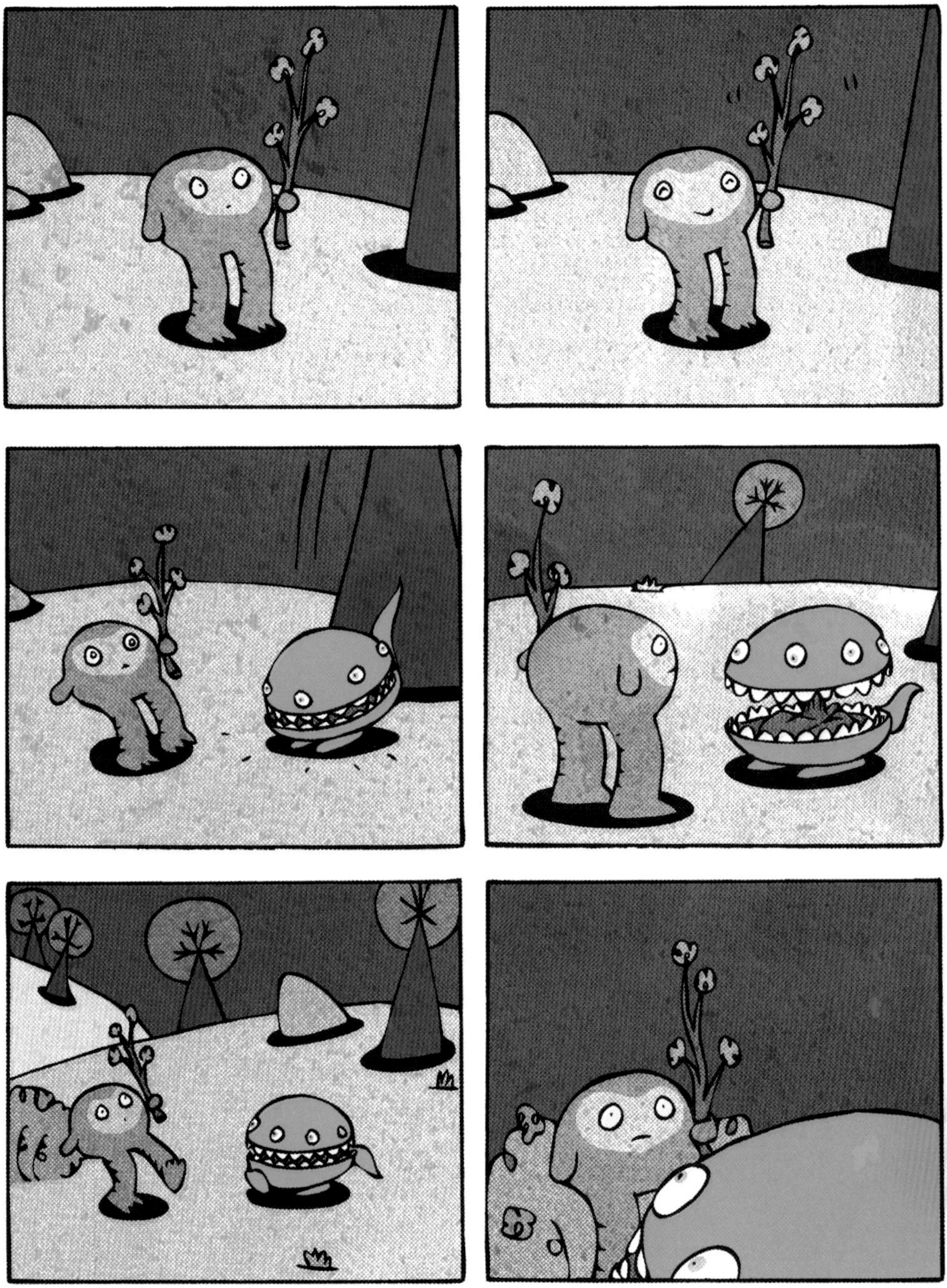

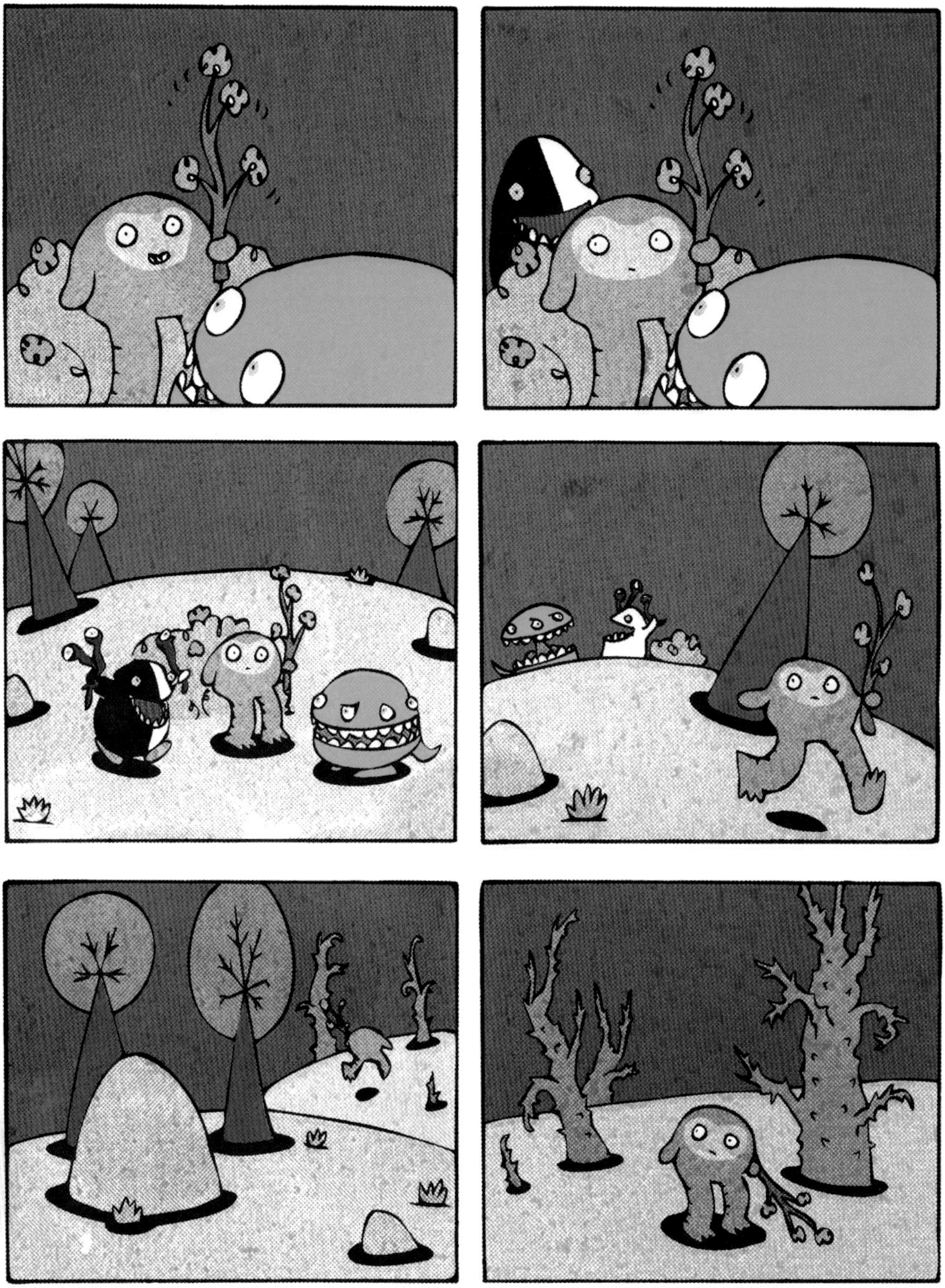

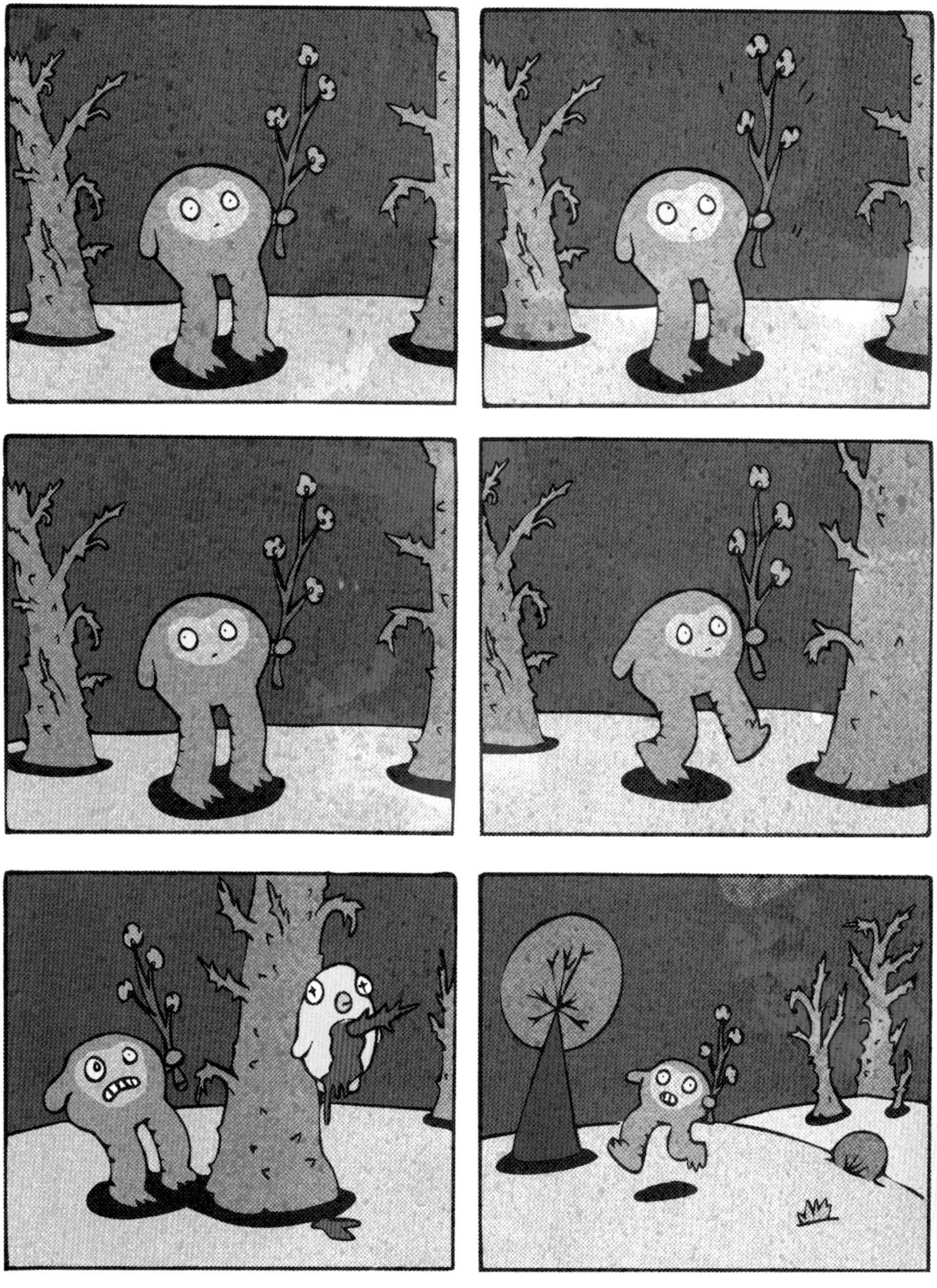

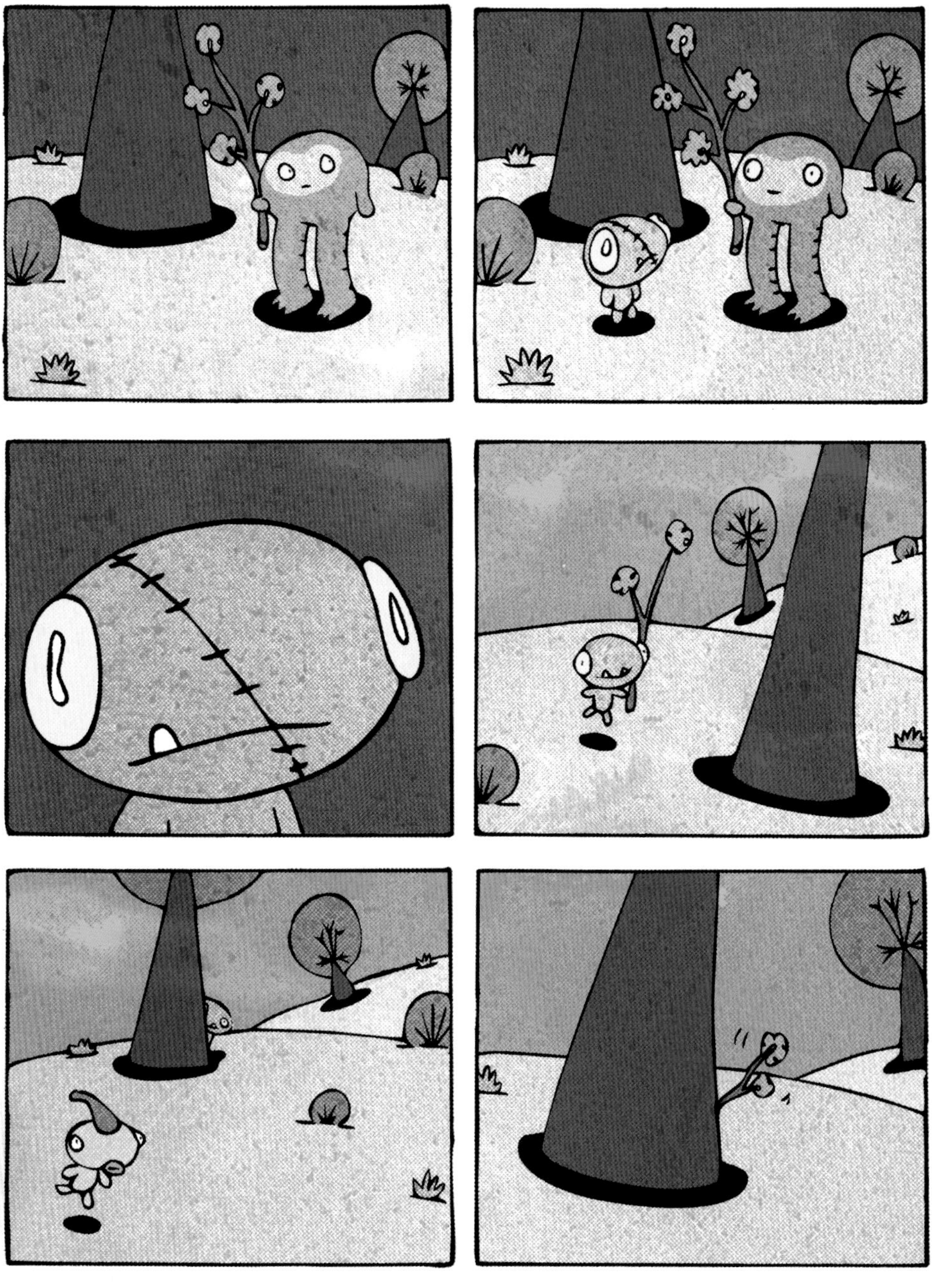

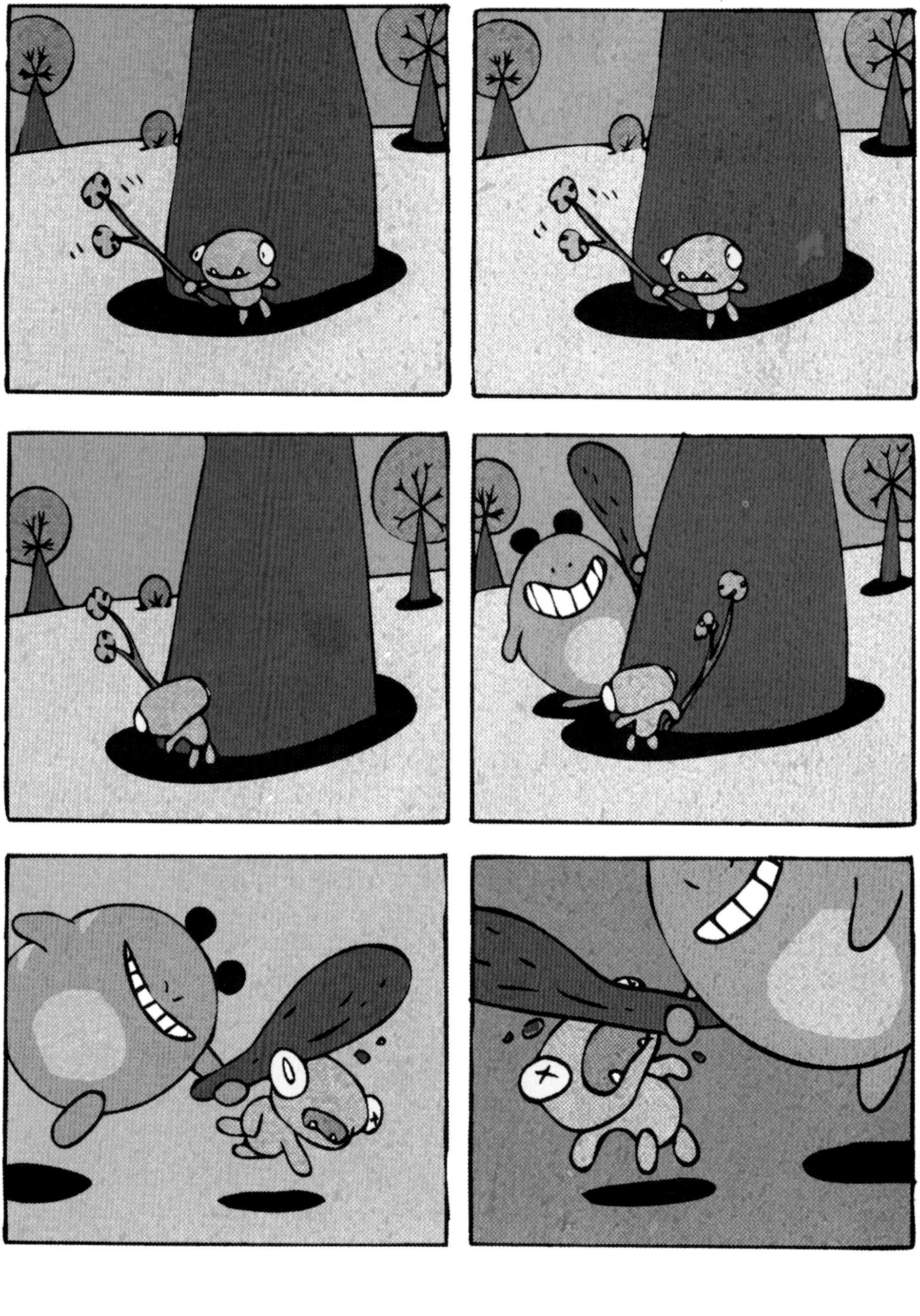

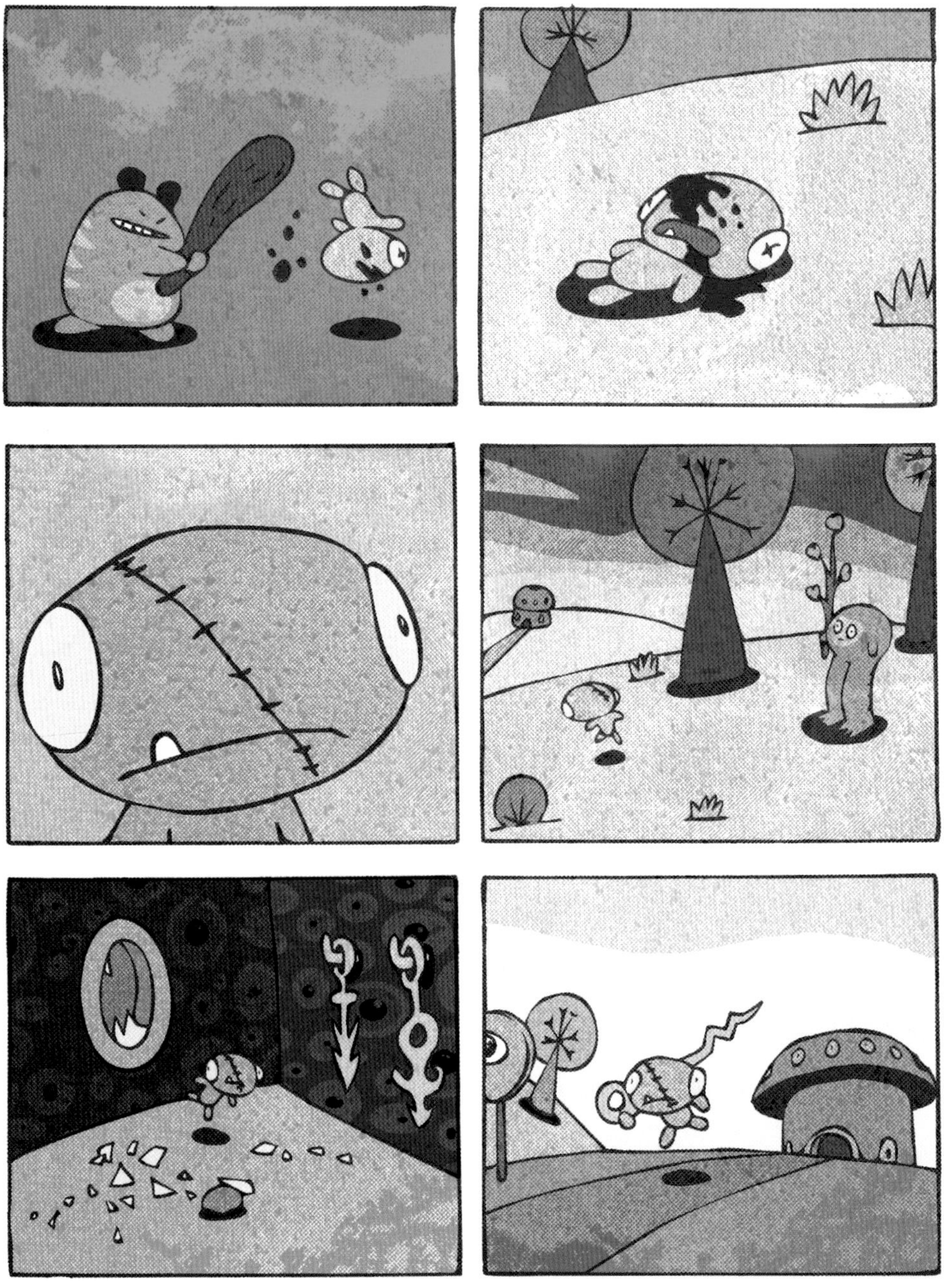

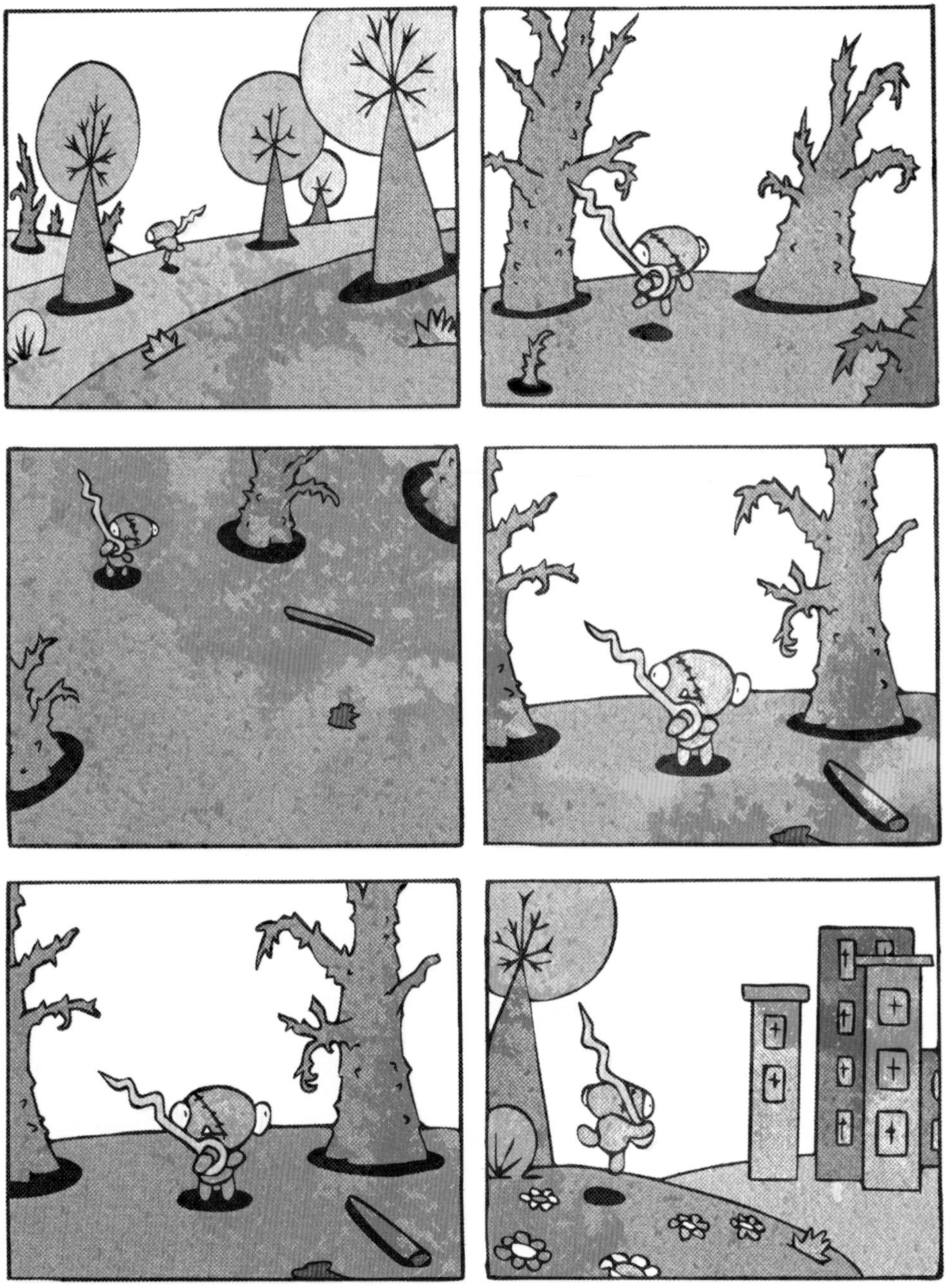

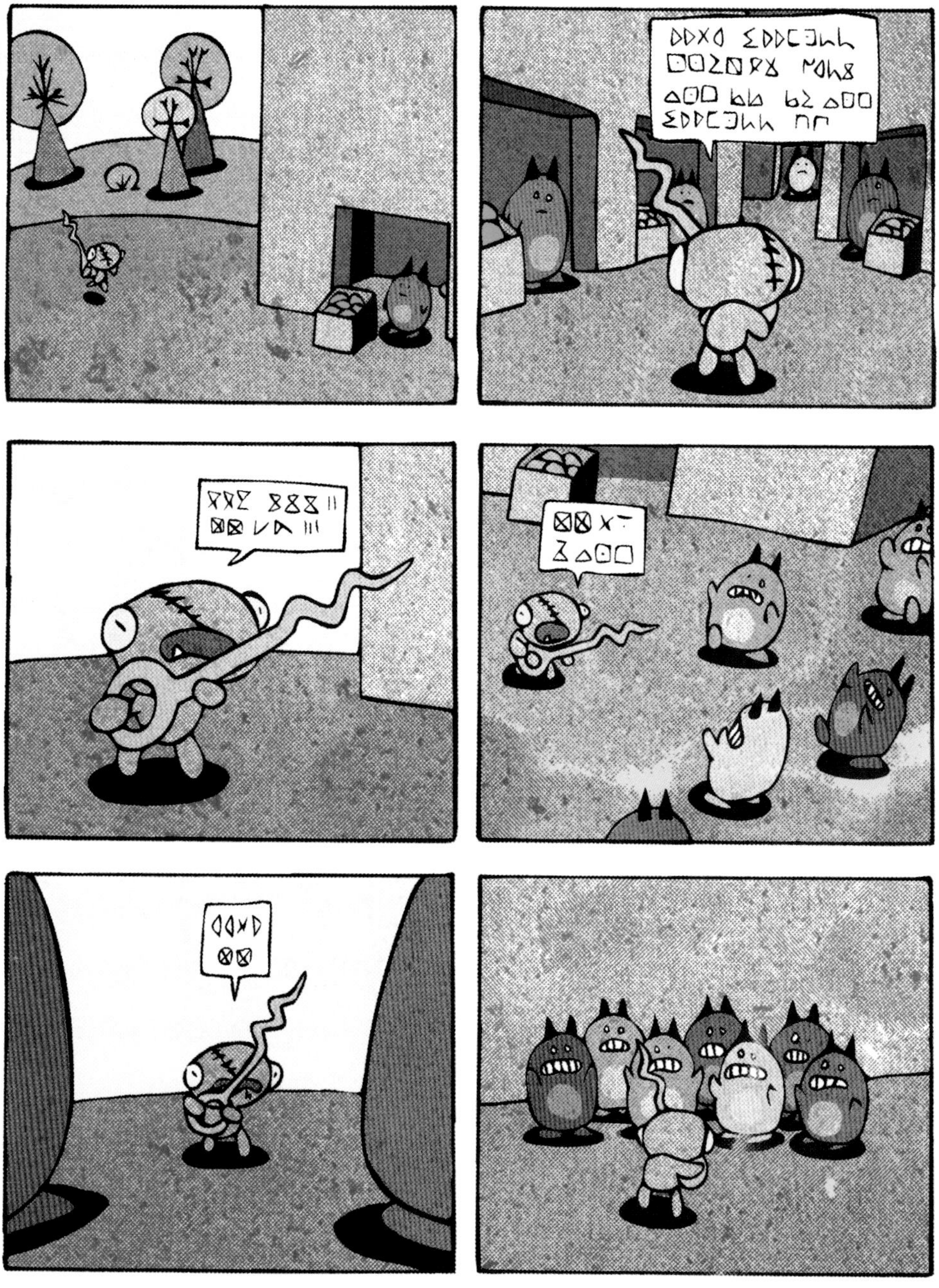

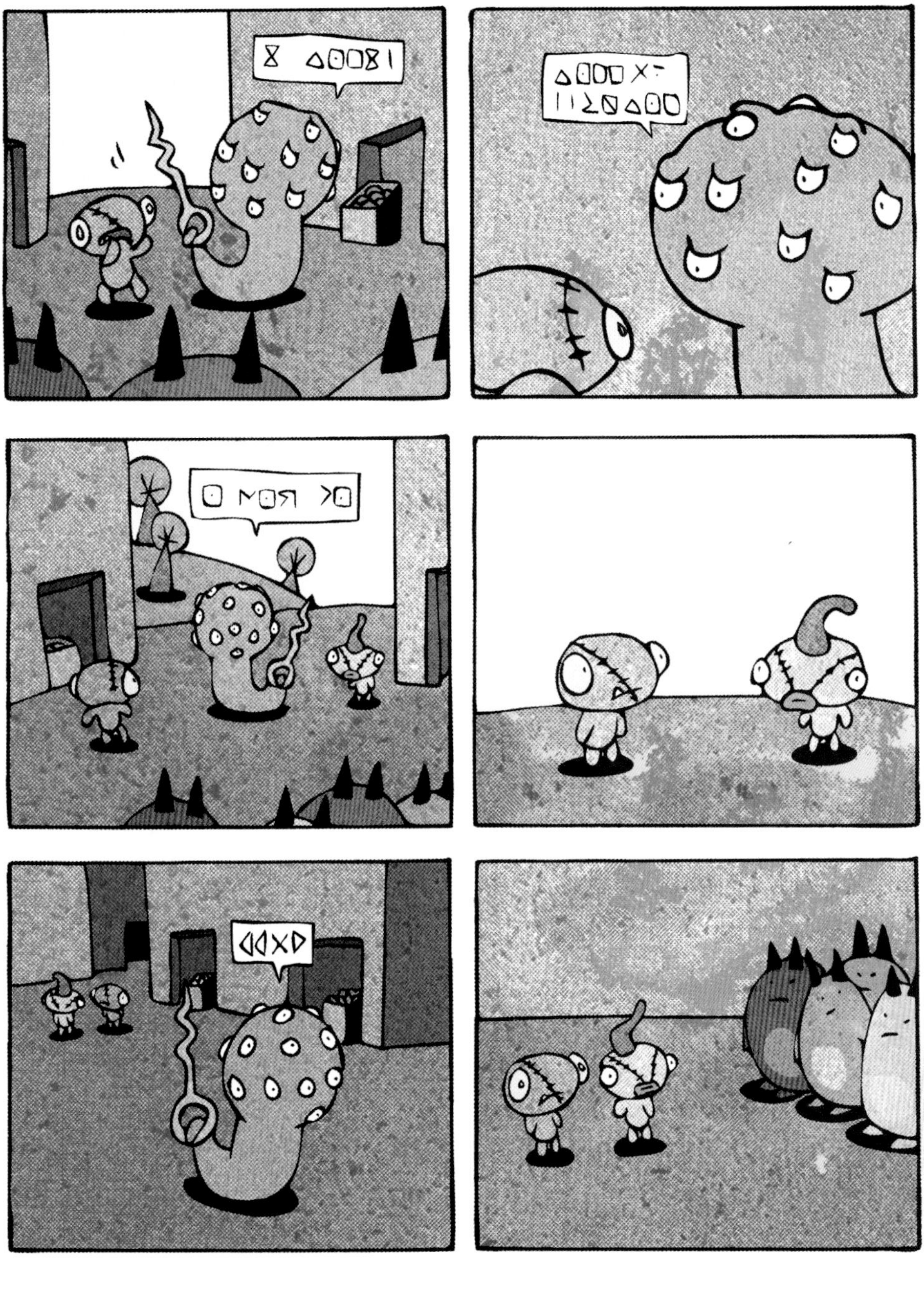

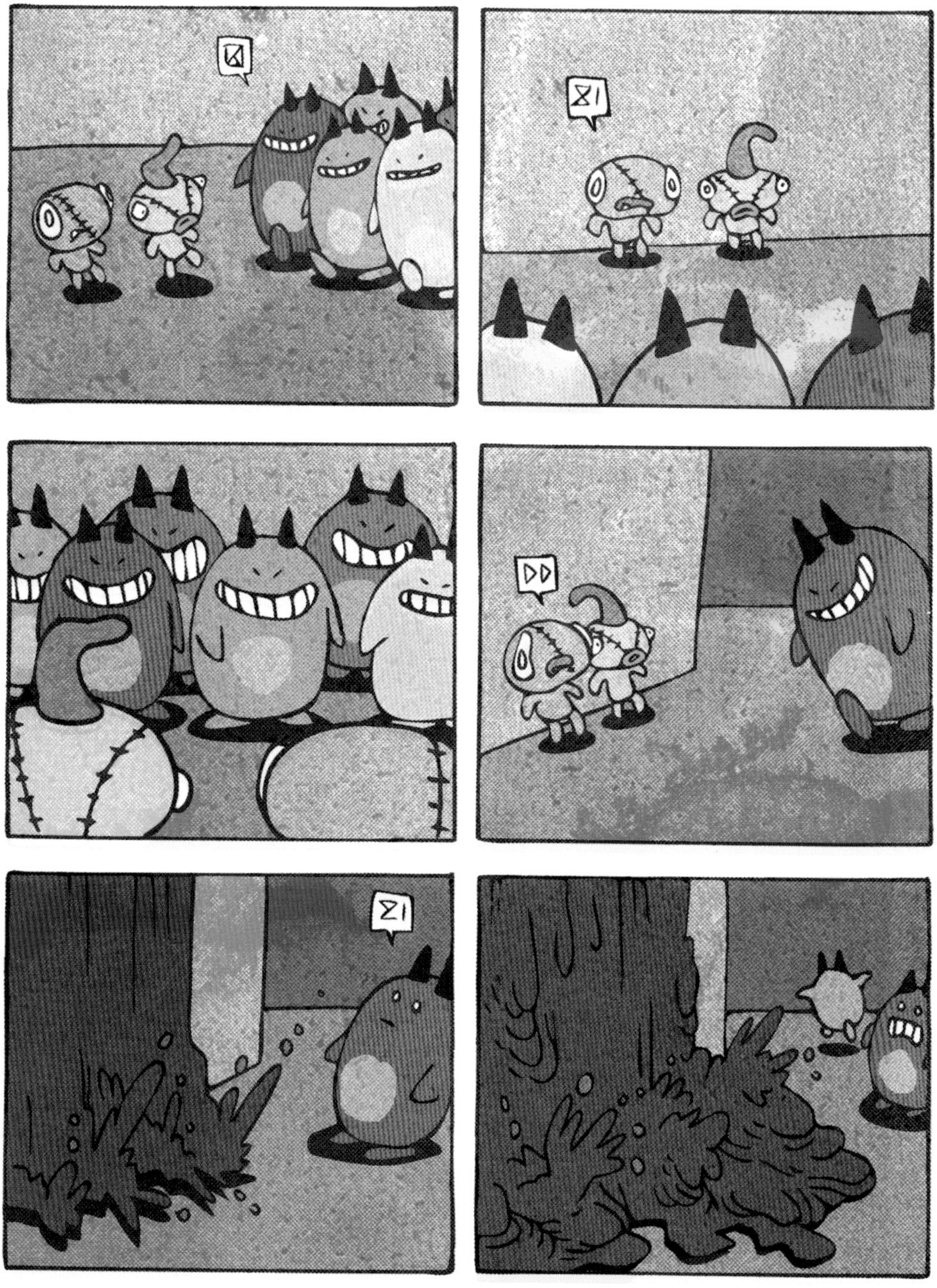

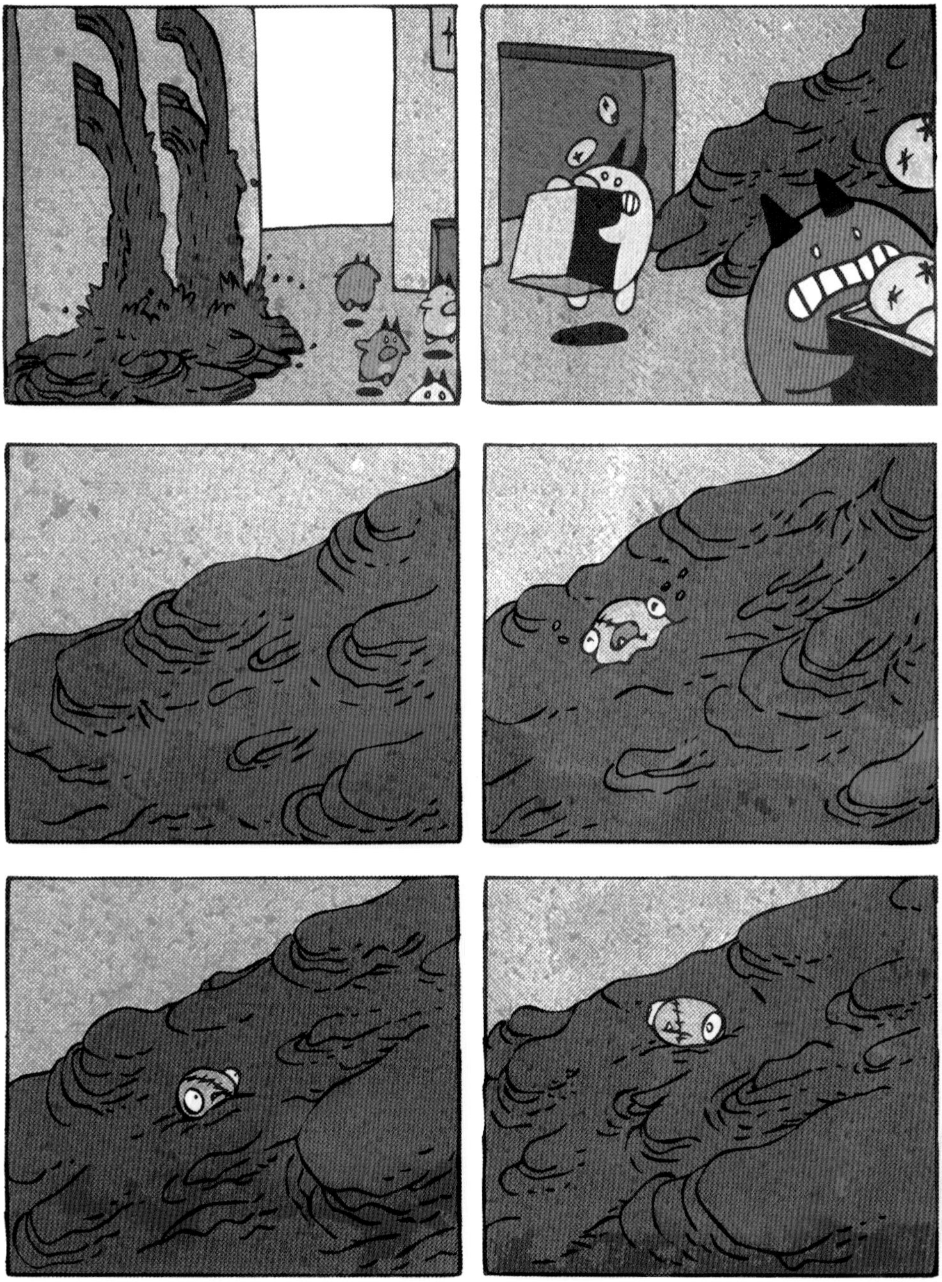

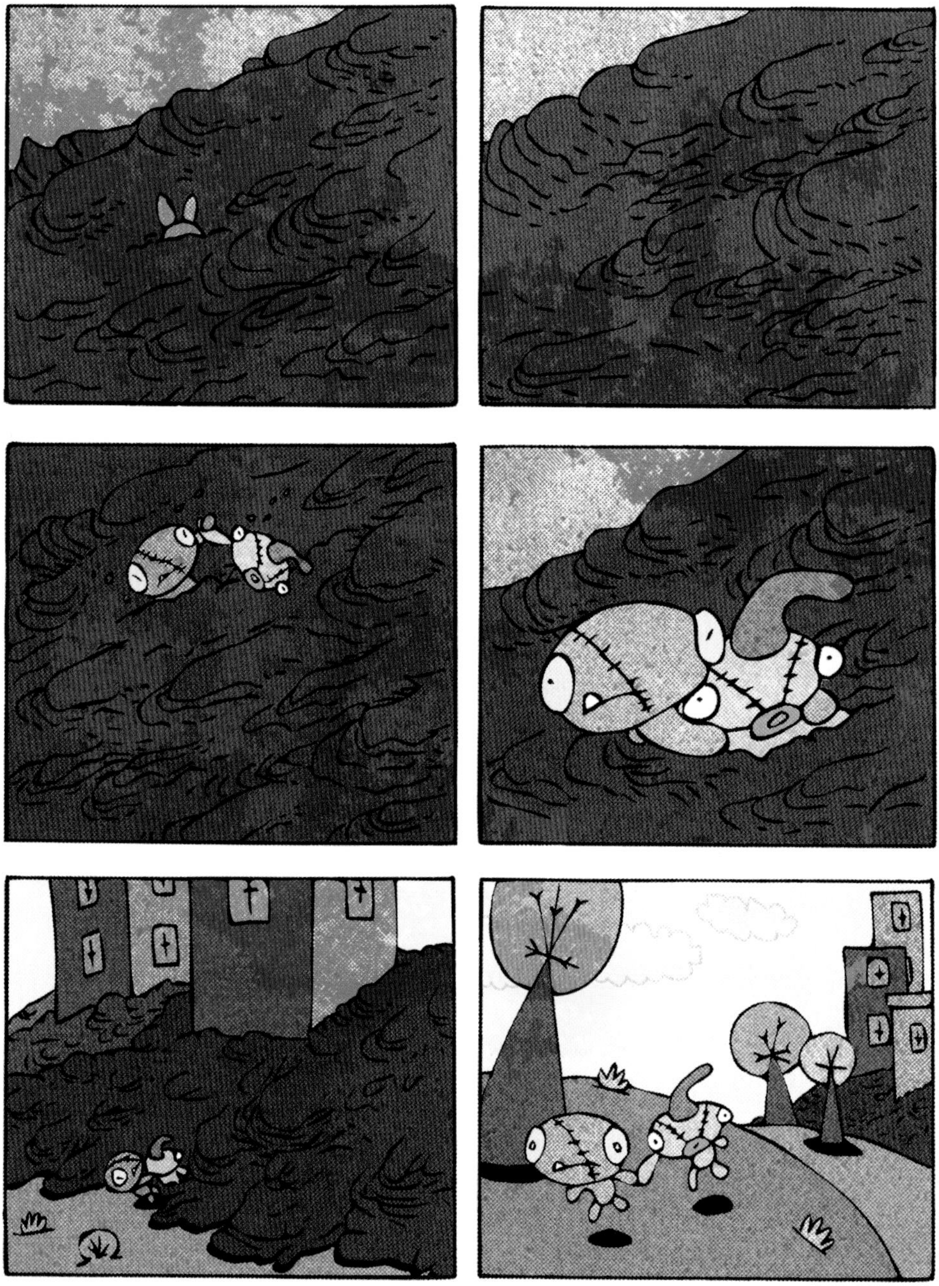

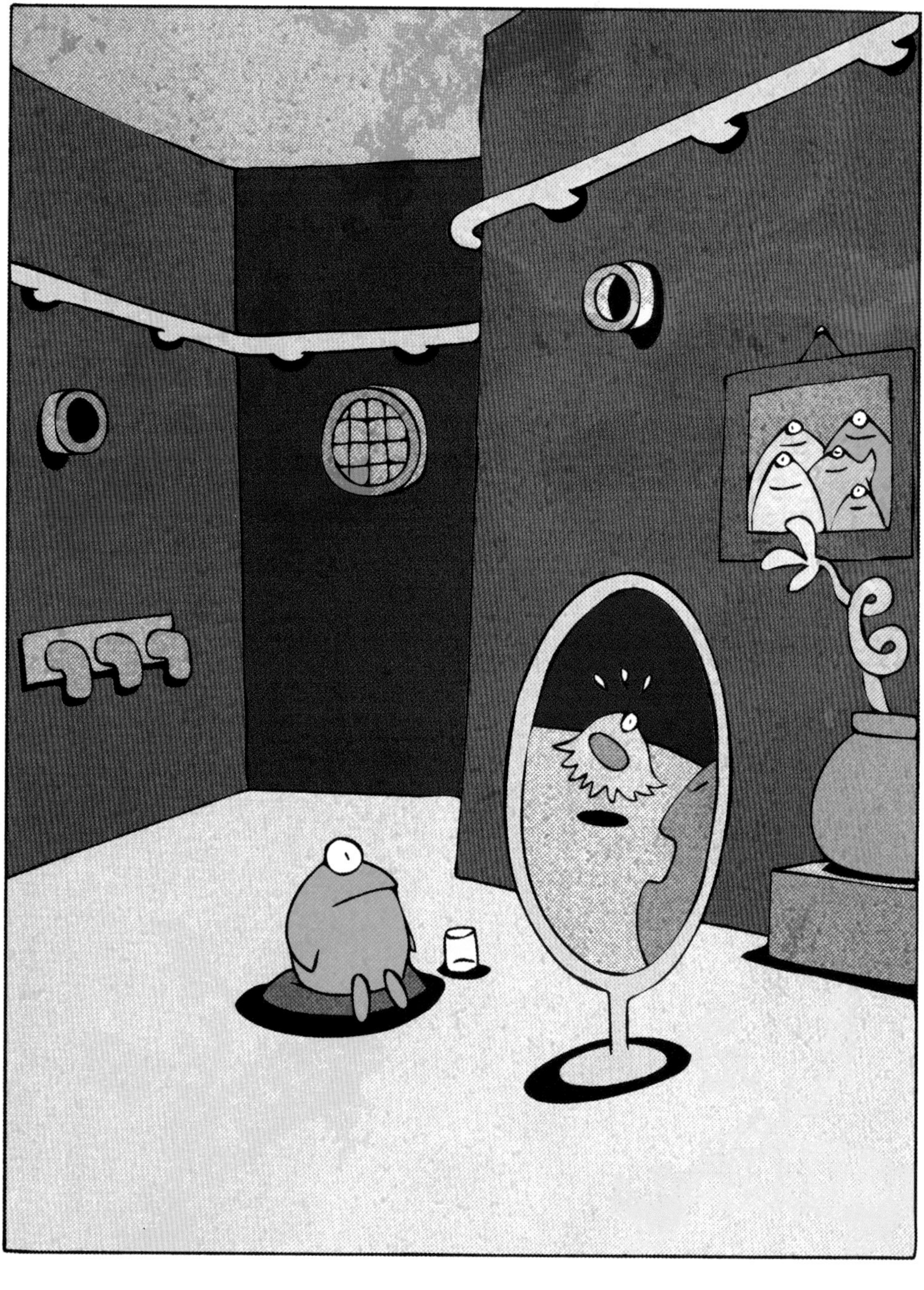

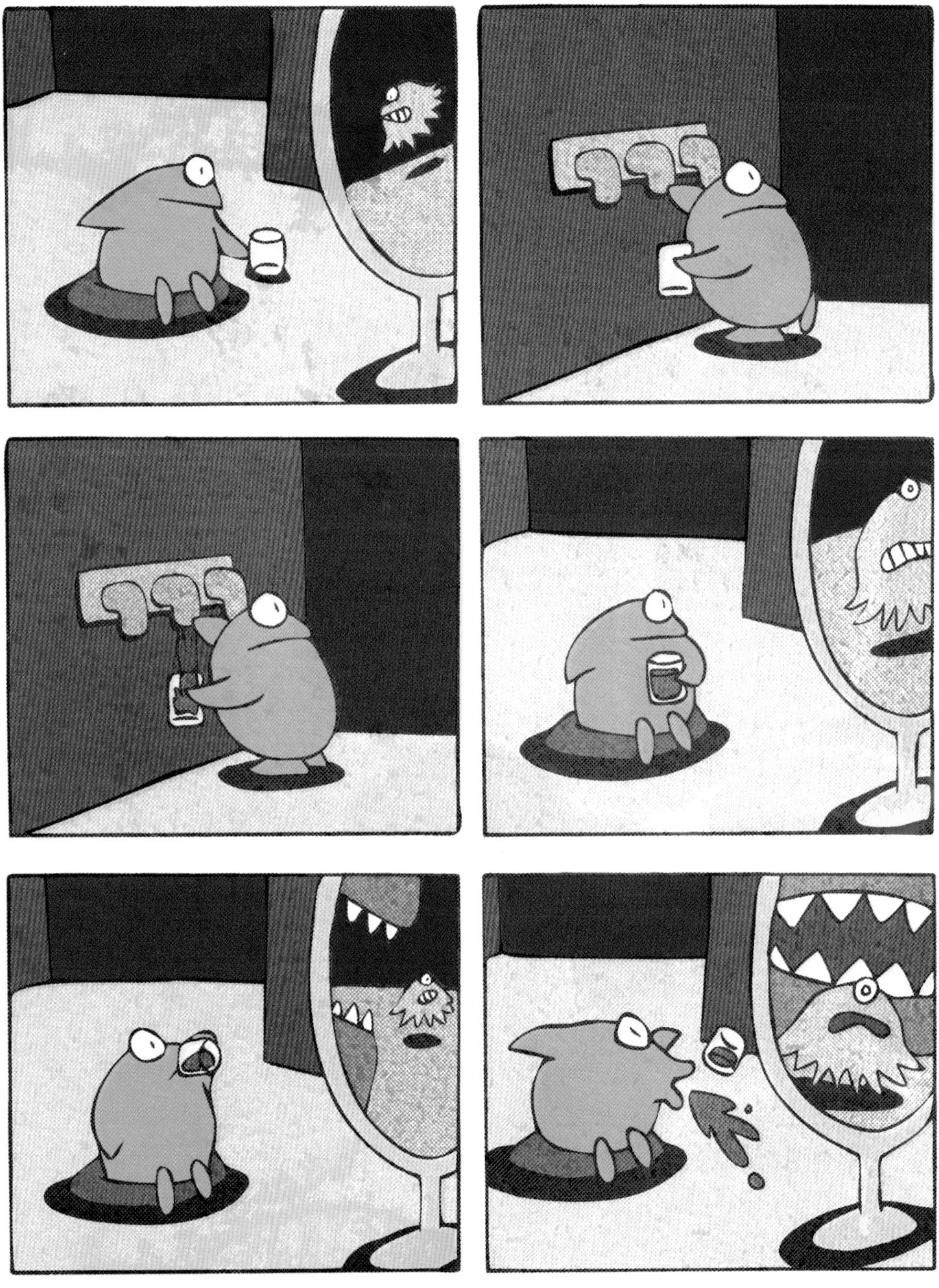

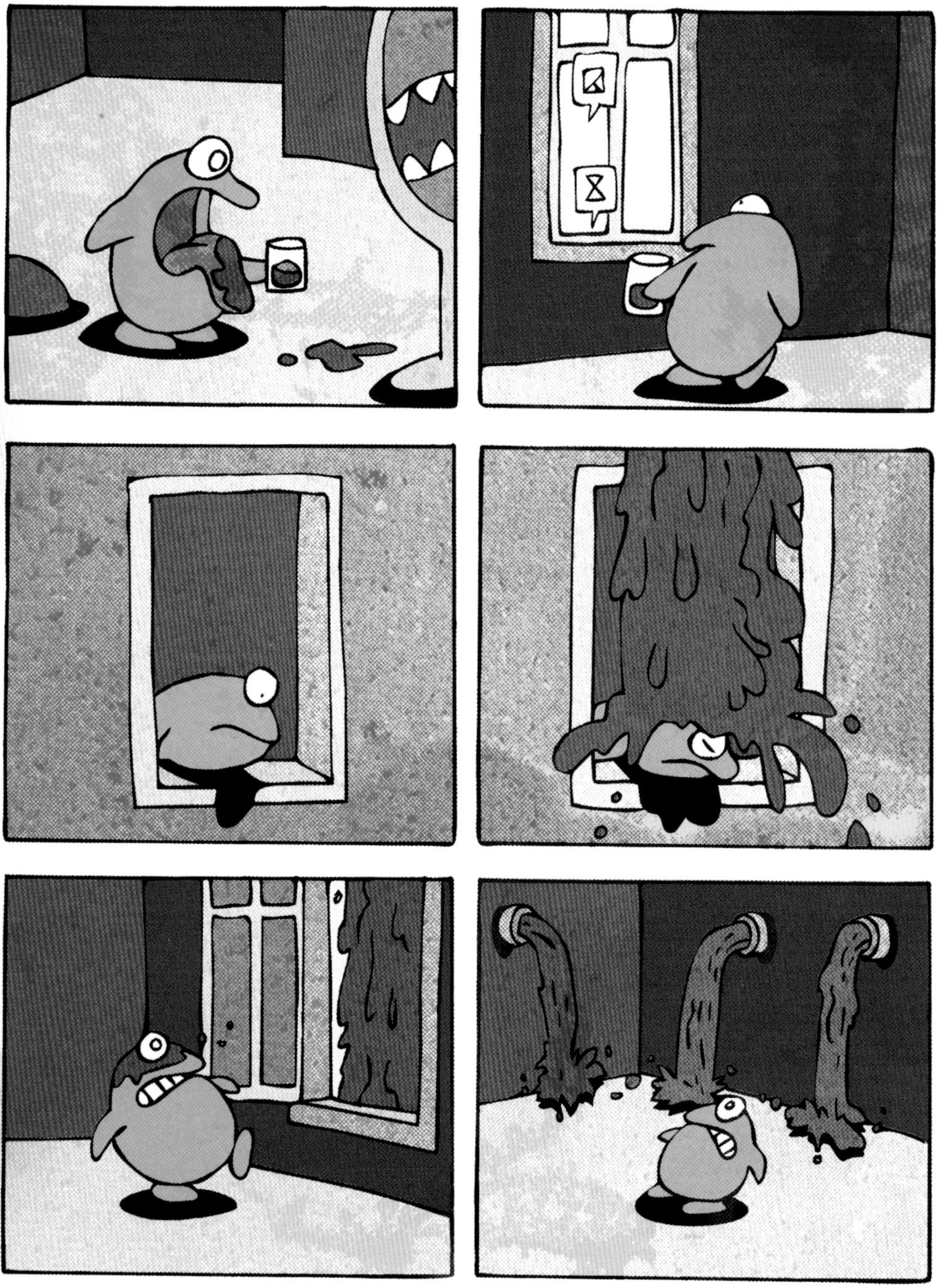

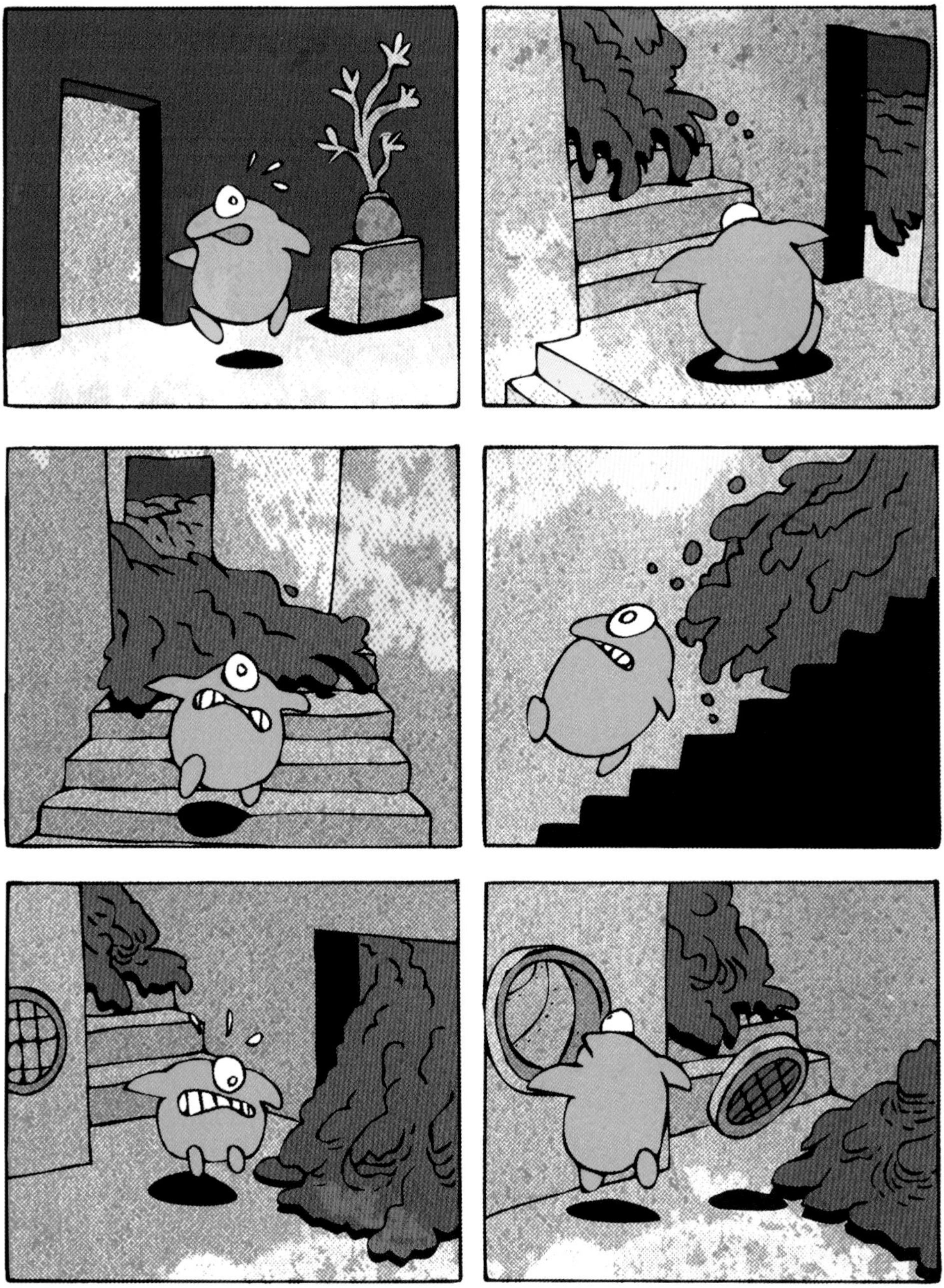

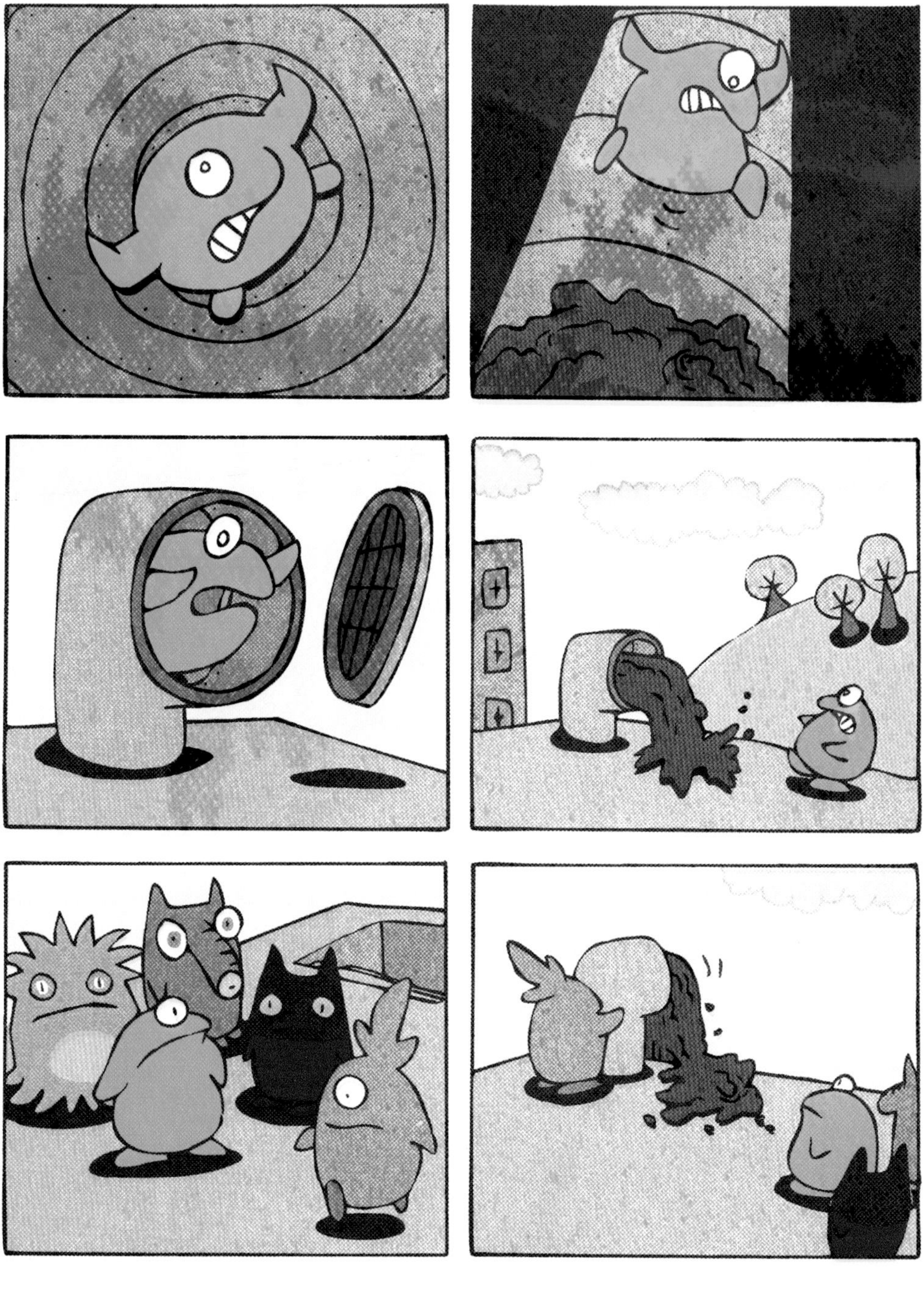

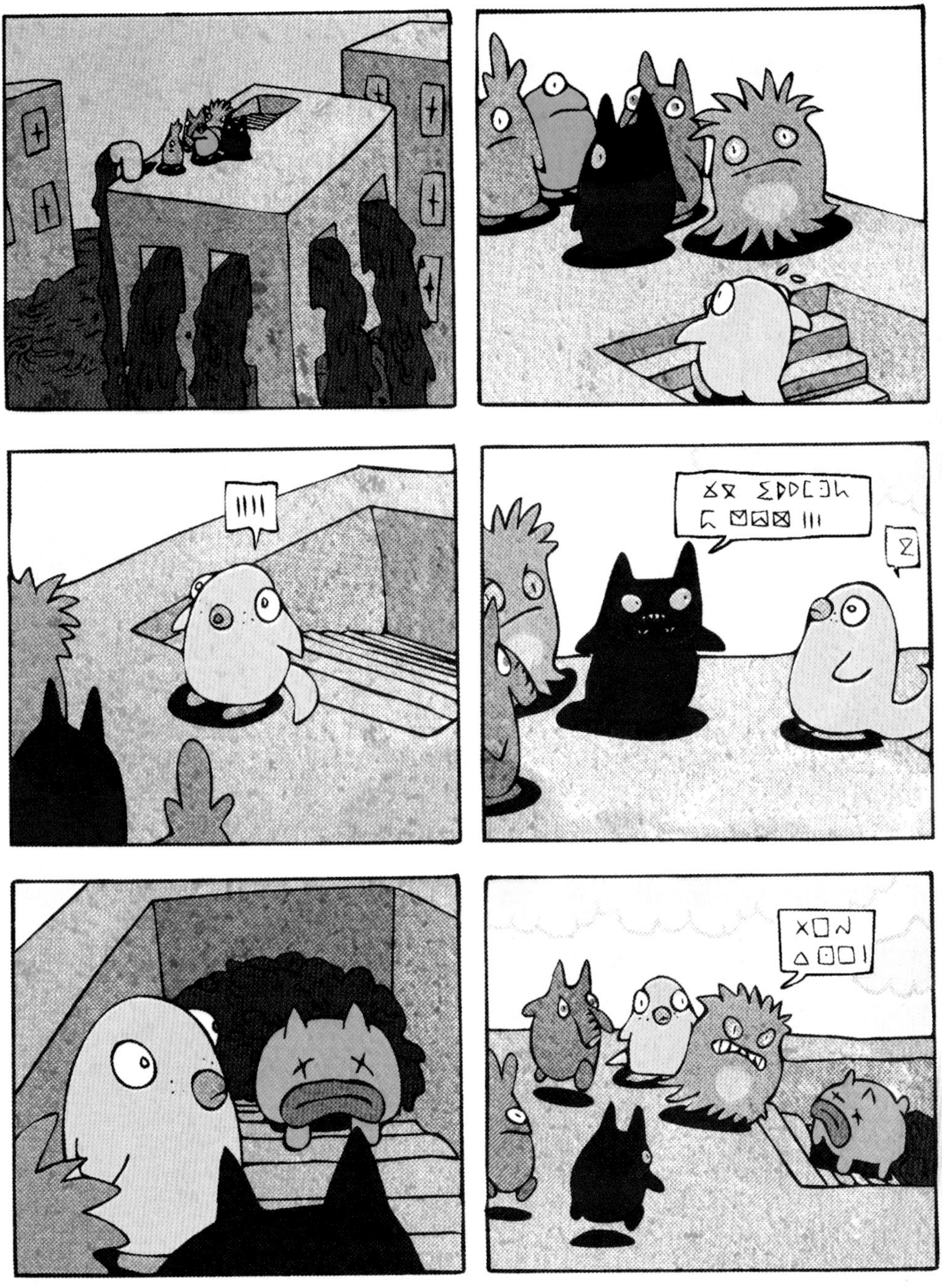

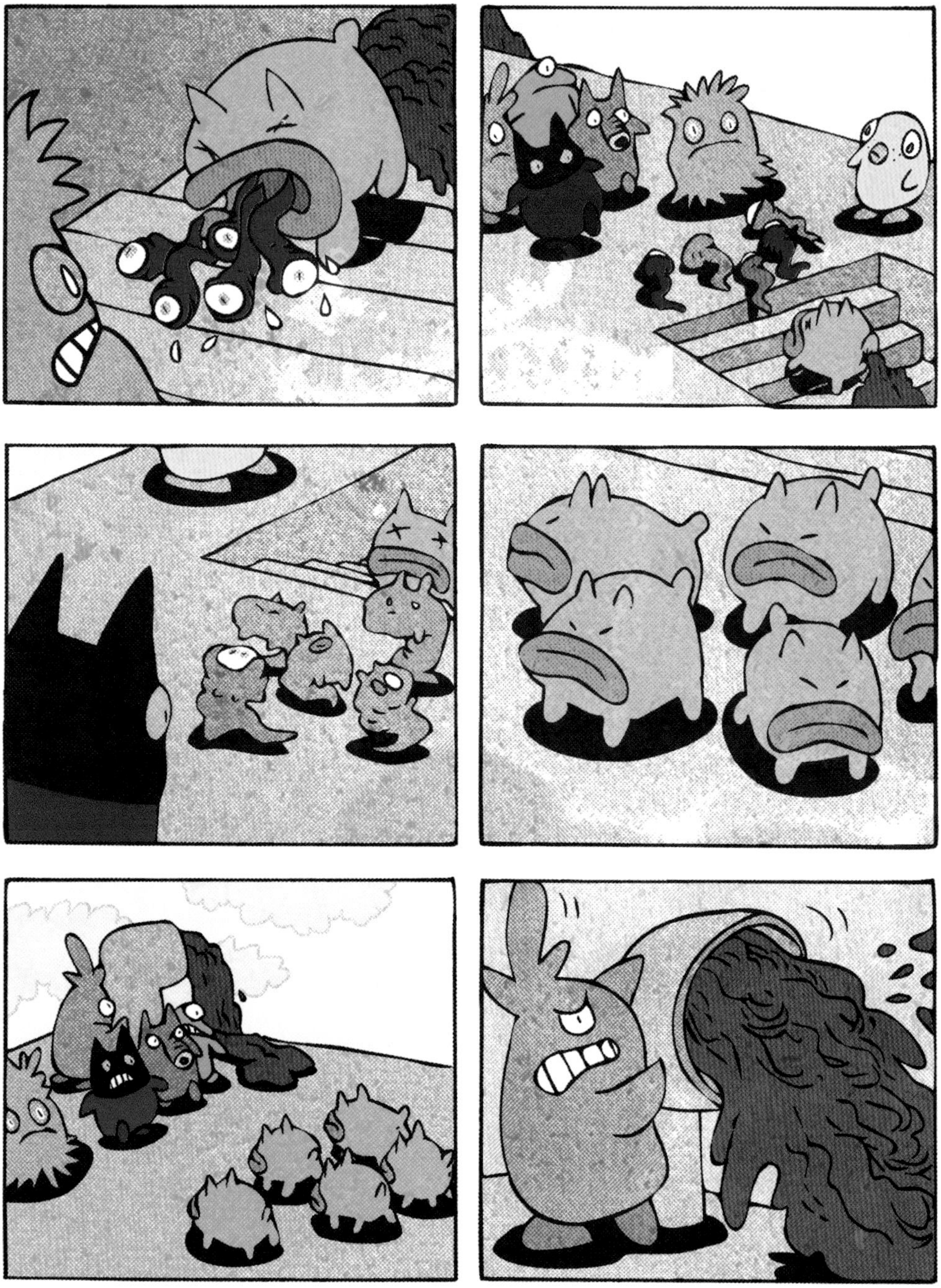

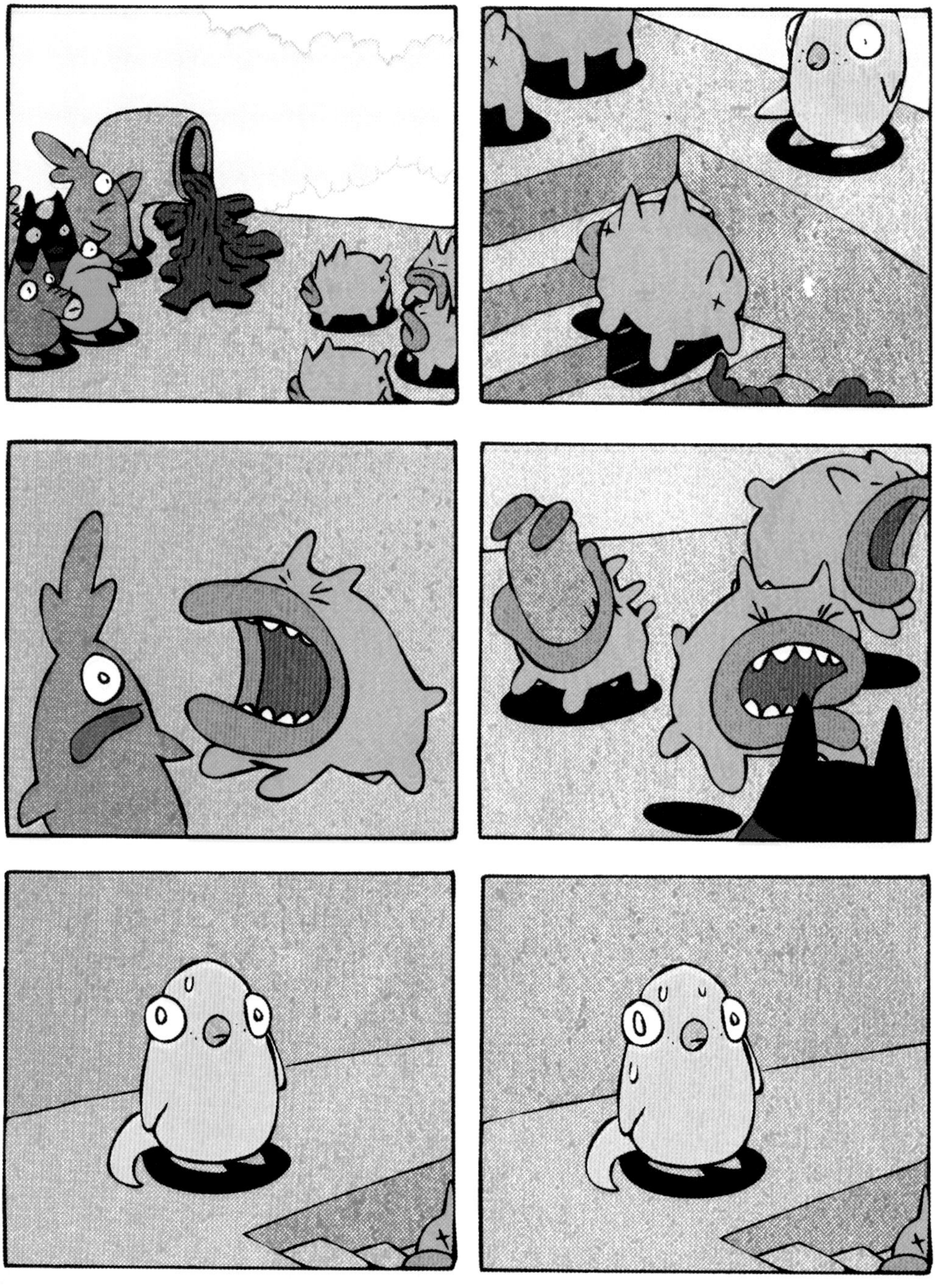

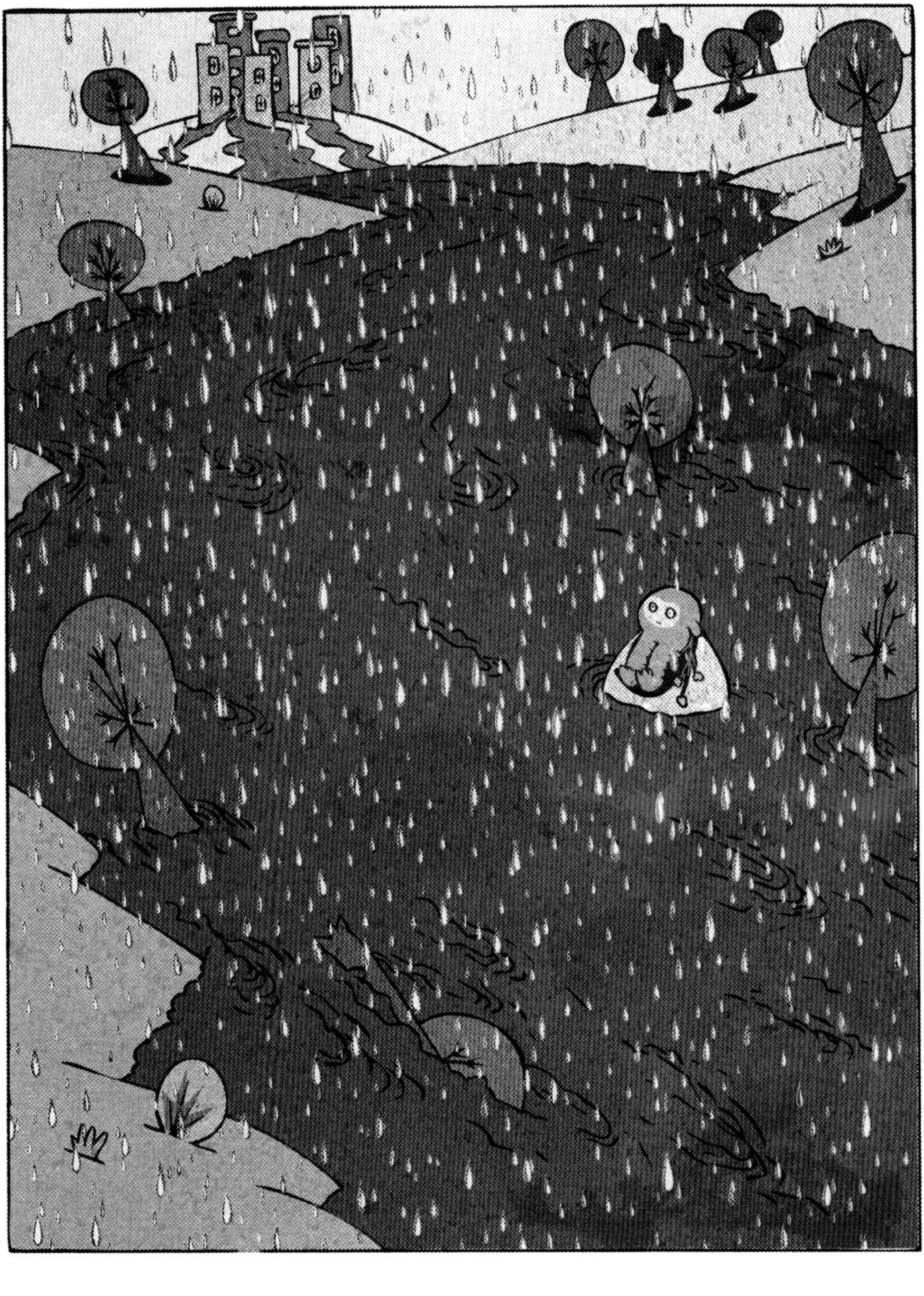

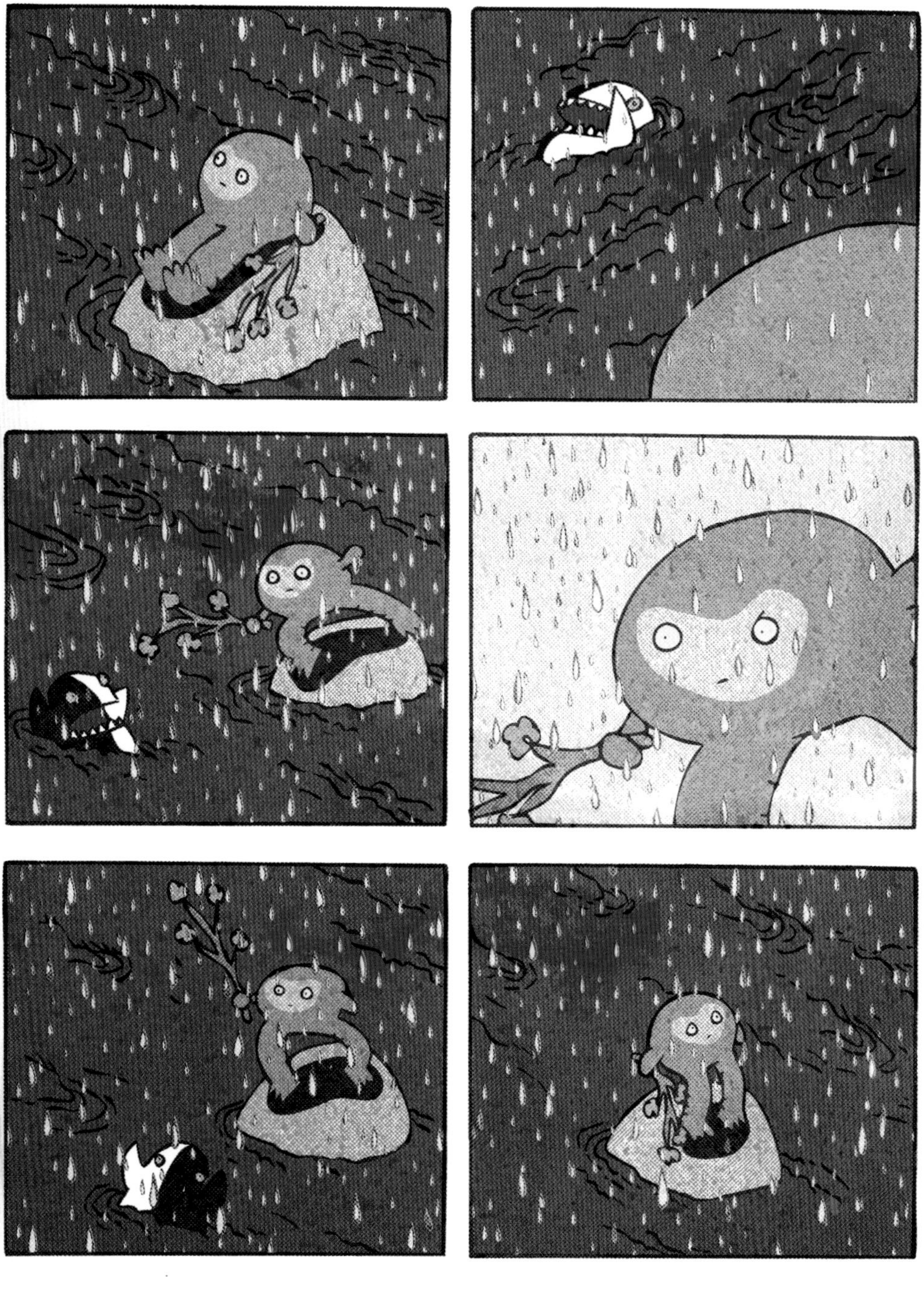

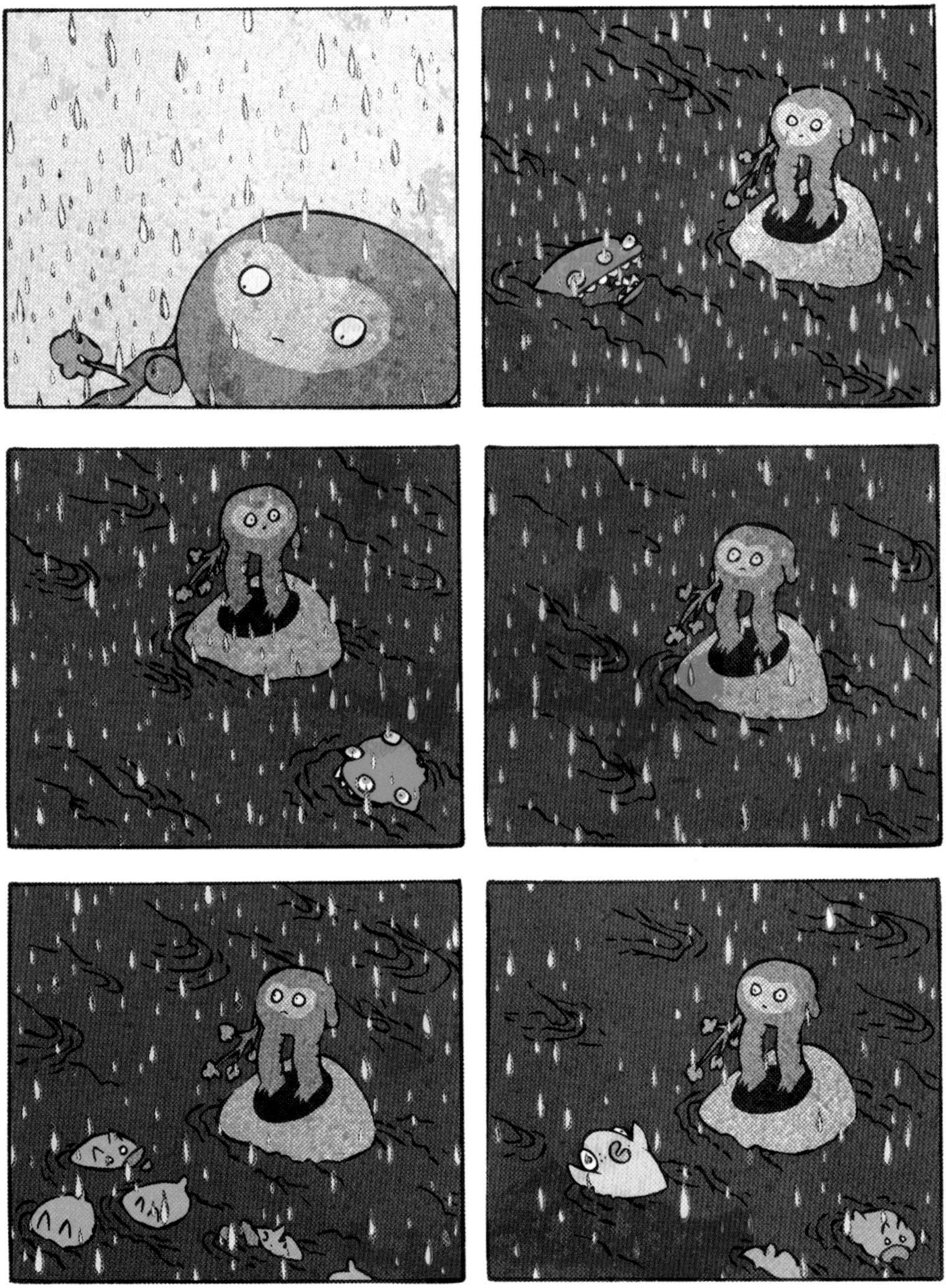

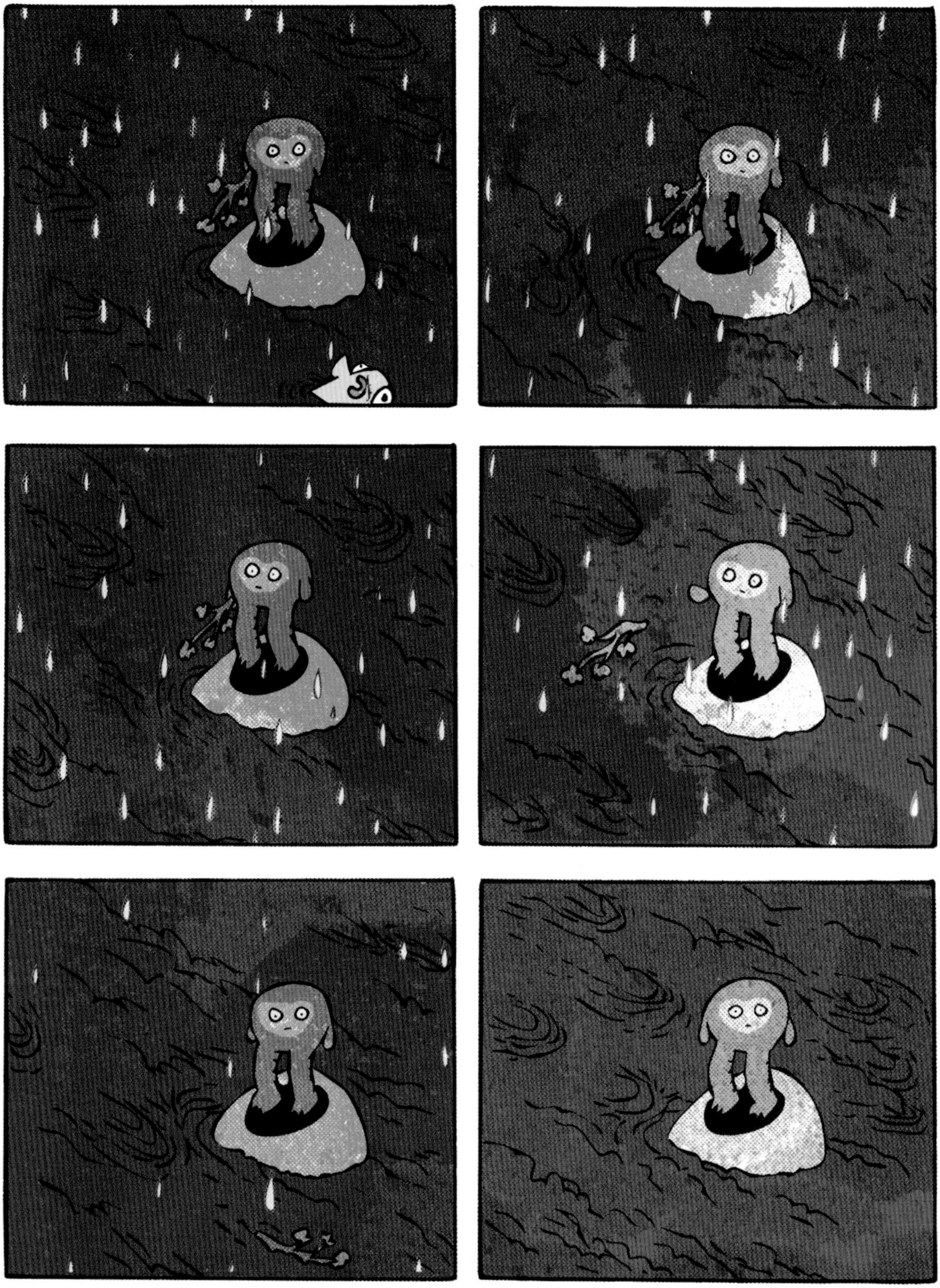

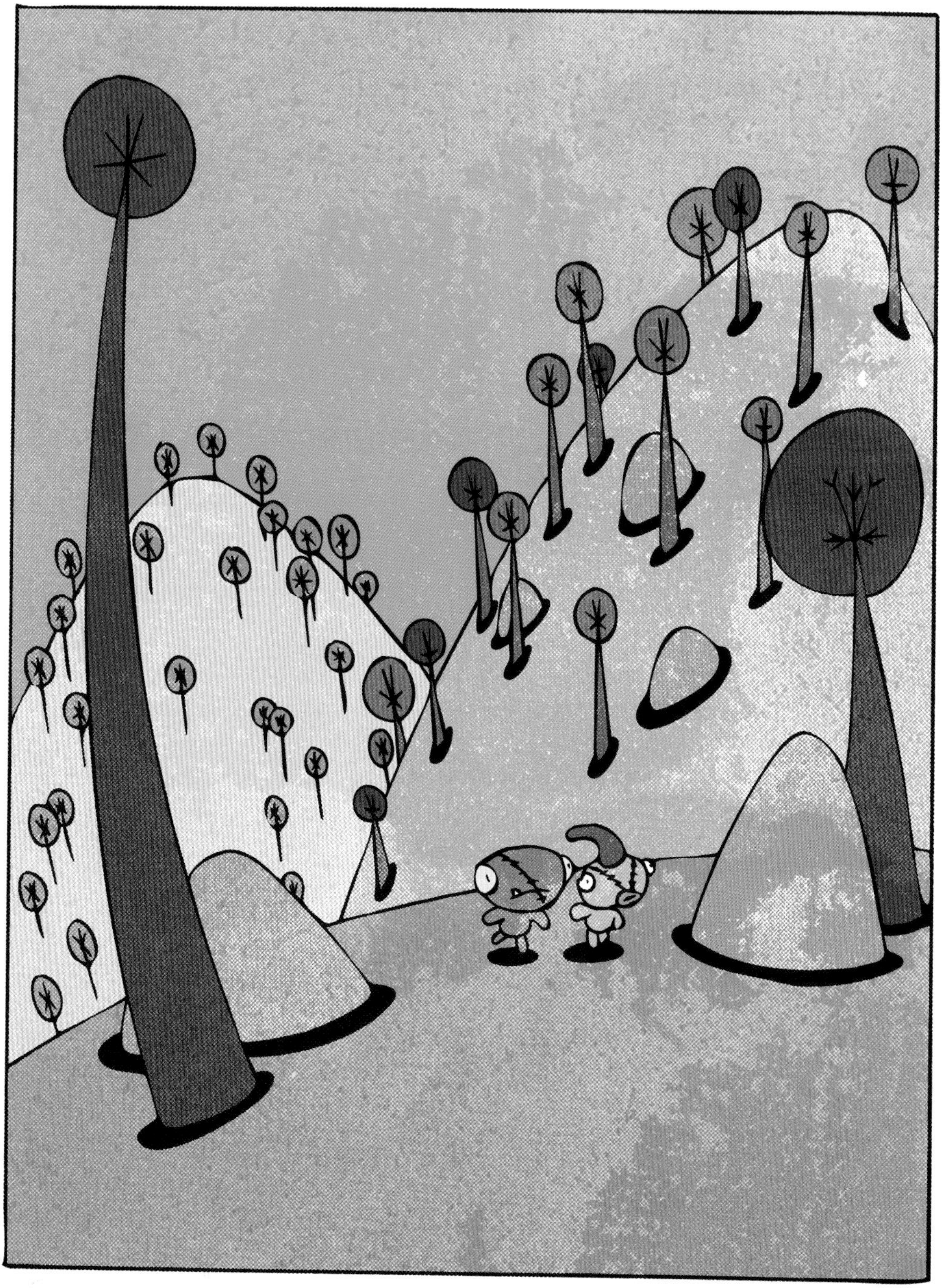

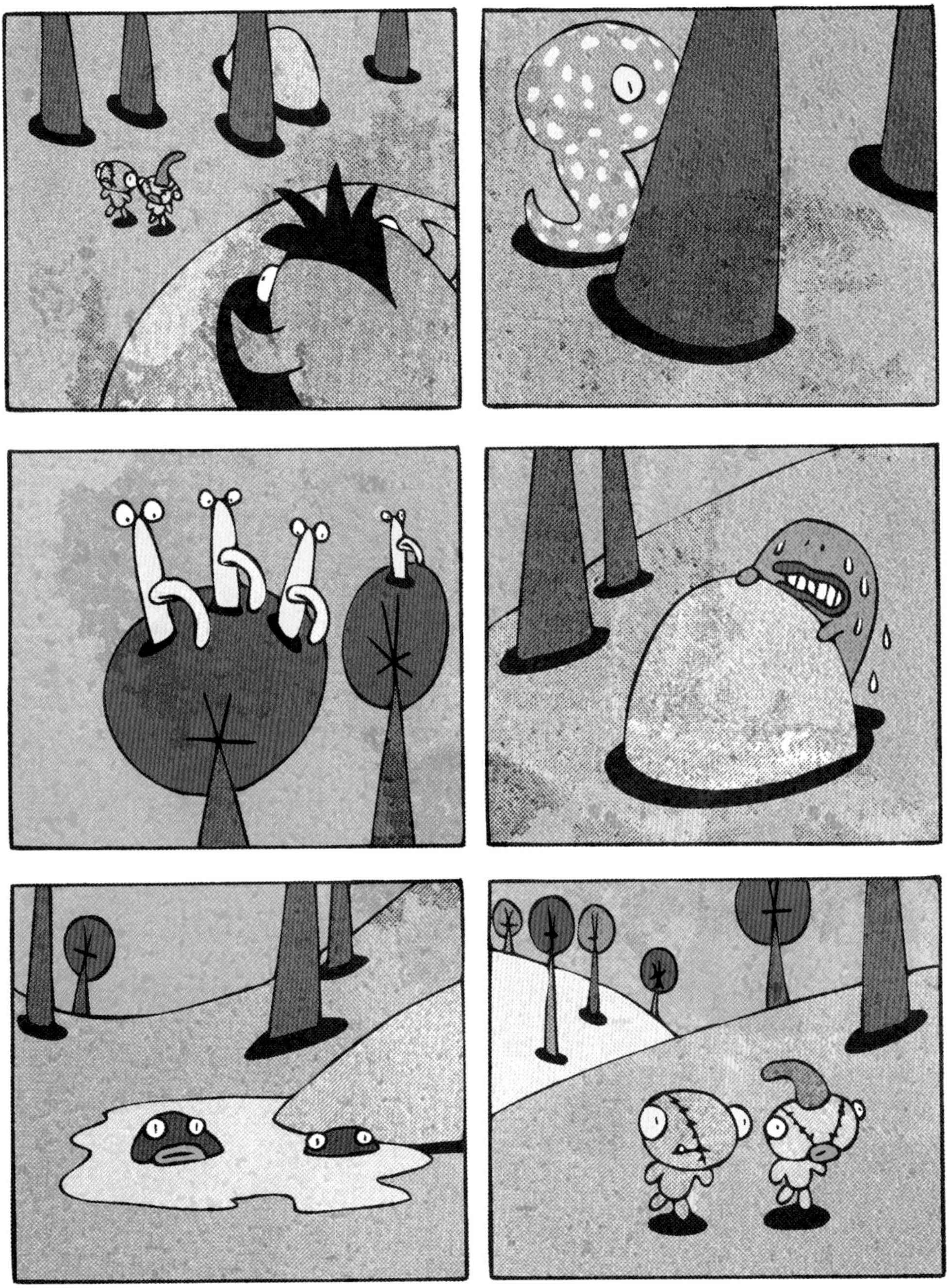

First Second

Published by First Second
First Second is an imprint of Roaring Brook Press, a division of
Holtzbrinck Publishing Holdings Limited Partnership
175 Fifth Avenue, New York, NY 10010

Distributed in Canada by H. B. Fenn and Company Ltd.
Distributed in the United Kingdom by Macmillan Children's Books,
a division of Pan Macmillan.

Originally published in France in 2004 under the title *A.L.I.E.E.N.*
by Editions Bréal, Rosny-sous-Bois, France.

Designed by Danica Novgorodoff.
Jacket design and paper aging by Lissi Erwin.
Introduction translated by Mark Siegel, copyright © 2006 by First Second.

Library of Congress Cataloging-in-Publication Data

Trondheim, Lewis.
A.L.I.E.E.N., archives of lost issues and earthly editions of extraterrestrial
novelties / Lewis Trondheim.
p. cm.
ISBN-13: 978-1-59643-095-2
ISBN-10: 1-59643-095-8
1. Graphic novels. I. Title: Archives of lost issues and earthly editions of
extraterrestrial novelties. II. Title: ALIEEEN, archives of lost issues and earthly
editions of extraterrestrial novelties. III. Title.

PN6727.T76A65 2006
741.5'944—dc22

2005052644

First Second books are available for special promotions and premiums.
For details, contact: Director of Special Markets, Holtzbrinck Publishers.

First American Edition April 2006

Printed in China

10 9 8 7 6 5 4 3 2